STAR WARS®

MILLENNIUM FALCON

Haynes

Modified YT-1300 Corellian Freighter

Owner's Workshop Manual

Ryder Windham

Illustrated by **Chris Reiff** and **Chris Trevas**

CONTENTS

THE HISTORY OF CORELLIAN ENGINEERING & THE YT-SERIES

THE HISTORY OF CORELLIAN ENGINEERING & THE YT-SERIES

Corellian Engineering Corporation (CEC) is arguably the best-known starship manufacturing company in the known galaxy. Also one of the oldest manufacturers, CEC was founded by a consortium of Corellia's best designers and shipbuilders in the early days of the Old Republic, when captains of small Corellian starships risked their lives to explore and map out safe routes through hyperspace. Unlike primary competitors Kuat Drive Yards and Sienar Fleet Systems, CEC does not rely heavily on military contracts, and remains primarily dedicated to the civilian market.

CEC is headquartered in the Corellian system, home of a remarkable number of highly skilled starship designers, engineers, and legendary starpilots. CEC's orbital shipyards produce a wide range of commercial vehicles for exploration, combat, and transporting passengers or freight. Ancillary CEC companies build escape pods, weapons and defense systems, and a multitude of optional add-ons for starships.

CEC built their reputation on starships that are fast, durable, and easily modifiable to suit the needs of independent operators and small companies. For centuries, the most popular testament to this reputation was CEC's YG-series light freighter. Long regarded as the backbone of intergalactic trade and commerce, a few antique YG freighters remain in use, but none resemble the original stock models, let alone each other. Because CEC has always encouraged owners to customize their purchase for individual needs, modifications are practically inevitable for any CEC starship.

Despite the popularity of CEC starships and the YG-series in particular, CEC's starship line was sometimes regarded as uninspired. Working with CEC marketing executives, CEC designers and shipbuilding specialists conceived a new series of ships that would be an affordable and even more modifiable alternative to the steadfast YG-series. In a rare instance of cross-company collaboration, CEC enlisted design help from Narro Sienar, owner of Santhe/Sienar Technologies, a chief competitor in the shipbuilding business. The result was the YT-series.

The YT-series revolutionized the interstellar shipping industry through its unparalleled application of modular design. The common characteristic of all YT-series ships was that they were built around a modifiable circular main corridor, with numerous options for modular compartments that could be positioned around the corridor, radiating out from a central core. A cockpit with large windows was usually mounted on the side of the ship, but was located on the top in some models. Each ship was enveloped by a saucer-shaped hull, to which a wide variety of components could be secured.

Because entire sections and compartments could be mass-produced and arranged into different configurations as required without extensive retooling, CEC not only saved an enormous amount of money, but was able to market the YT-series at extremely competitive prices. Thousands of YT-series ships were produced, and no two were exactly alike.

In the decades that followed the release of the first YT ships, the Old Republic fell to the Galactic Empire. Like other manufacturers, CEC did build starships that were either commissioned or appropriated by the Imperial Navy; but when the Rebel Alliance rose up against the Empire, CEC donated ships and supplies to the Rebels.

And in two decisive battles, a privately owned Corellian Engineering Corporation YT-1300 freighter named the *Millennium Falcon* helped shape the course of history.

⇐ The YT-1300 light freighter *Millennium Falcon* and the
YT-2400 light freighter *Outrider* leaving the planet Tatooine.

Despite Corellian Engineering Corporation's reputation for innovation, it did not envision the YT-1000 transport as a bold new direction in starship design but as an experimental departure from the YG series and a possible replacement for CEC's venerable Barloz-class freighters. Although the larger Barloz freighters were still in demand by independent merchants and some planetary defense forces, CEC executives and designers had begun to see the large, somewhat wedge-shaped Barloz as 'tired'.

CEC designers and technicians were keen to incorporate new technology into the YT-1000, but they also turned to the past for design inspiration. Ancient holograms yielded images and partial data and schematics for a CEC XS stock light freighter that was in use during the Great Galactic War. The XS freighter had an aft that resembled a halved saucer with a heavily armored hull, and the fore featured a blunt cockpit with a narrow viewport that jutted forward from the ship's center. CEC designers became excited over the prospect of a relatively small saucer-shaped freighter that might be engineered to have almost the same amount of cargo capacity as a larger Barloz, but their partial data and schematics for the XS freighter left them questioning certain details. They consulted

Narro Sienar, an expert on ancient freighters who was then owner of Santhe/Sienar Technologies, and Sienar was by all accounts delighted to work with the CEC engineers.

The result of this design experiment was the YT-1000, which came equipped with sublight engines, a Class 3 hyperdrive, navicomputer, simple sensor suite, and a standard laser cannon. The stock model had limited modular options for the interior, but had a cargo capacity of 75 metric tons. In a slight nod to the ancient XS freighter, the YT-1000's cockpit was centered atop the ship's hull. Instead of a narrow viewport, the cockpit sported large transparisteel windows retrofitted from Barloz-class freighter cockpit canopies.

The YT-1000 was largely well received by customers, but after CEC marketing executives reviewed customer surveys, they decided a limited production run was for the best. In the surveys, nearly all the customers indicated they liked the design of the YT-1000, but that they would be willing to pay more for a larger ship that offered more modular options.

The YT-1000 was succeeded by the YT-1200 and YT-1210, which introduced a side-mounted cockpit to the YT series but were not otherwise significantly advanced.

⬇ Built by Corellian Engineering Corporation, the ancient XS stock light freighter (below) inspired the designers of the YT-1000. The XS itself was modeled after an even older ship, the *Dynamic*-class freighter built by Core Galaxy Systems during the Jedi Civil War.

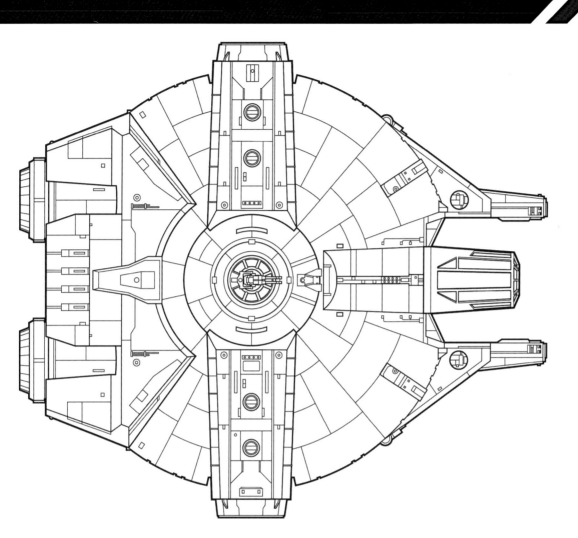

SPECIFICATIONS

CRAFT: YT-1000
LENGTH: 28m
MAXIMUM SPEED (atmosphere): 740kph (460mph)
HYPERDRIVE: Class 3
HYPERDRIVE BACKUP: Class 16
SHIELDING: Equipped

NAVIGATION SYSTEM: Navicomputer
ARMAMENT: 1 standard laser cannon
CREW: 2
PASSENGERS: 4
CARGO: 75 metric tons
CONSUMABLES: 2 months
COST: 85,000 (20,000 used)

CEC upgraded their unsold YT-1200 and YT-1210 ships, and marketed them as a 'new' model number, the YT-1250, which was released after the YT-1300. See page 22.

Of all the transports manufactured by Corellian Engineering Corporation, the YT-1300 may best exemplify the design concept of an affordable, durable, and easily modifiable transport. Although CEC promotes the idea that each YT-1300 is unique because of modification options, production was initially dedicated to two standard configurations, which were designated the YT-1300f and YT-1300p, for 'freight' and 'passenger' respectively. Both YT-1300 configurations appear very similar on the outside, each having a saucer-shaped hull, forward mandibles, a starboard-mounted cockpit, and a single laser cannon; inside, each was equipped with a Quadex power core and Class 2.0 Corellian Avatar-10 hyperdrive and Class 12 backup hyperdrive. However, floor plans vary considerably because each ship was assembled to meet the demands of customers with individual tastes and requirements.

YT-1300p interior configuration has a minimal amount of cargo space and three passenger cabin modules. Cargo is limited to a single hold separated by the freight loading room. Each passenger cabin has three bunks, a compact refresher, and a storage

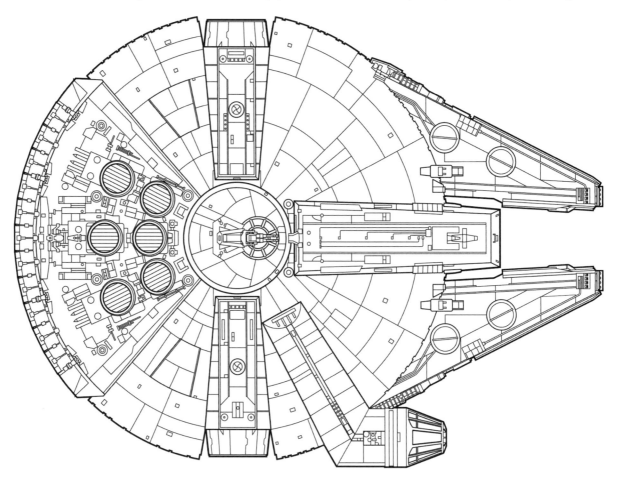

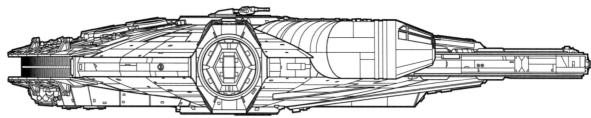

compartment. Although the slope of the cabin ceilings limited the headroom above the bunks located outermost from the ship's center, CEC conversion kits allowed the remaining bunks to be transformed into bunk beds for a total of five bunks per cabin. Crew accommodations consist of two bunks, which also can be converted into bunk beds, in the engineering bay, and a common refresher situated in the main corridor, across from the passenger lounge.

Instead of boarding ramps, the YT-1300p has two retractable boarding ladders that extend below the port and starboard passage tubes; passengers unable to climb the boarding ladders may enter the ship via an elevator in the engineering bay. When the boarding ladders are raised into the 'floor' position, the rungs automatically flatten against the deck so passengers can walk across them safely. Hatches separate the passage tubes from the ship's circular corridor, allowing the passage tubes to be used as airlocks. A Class-6 escape pod is located at the outermost end of each passage tube, and five single-occupant escape pods are located beneath floor hatches in the engineering bay.

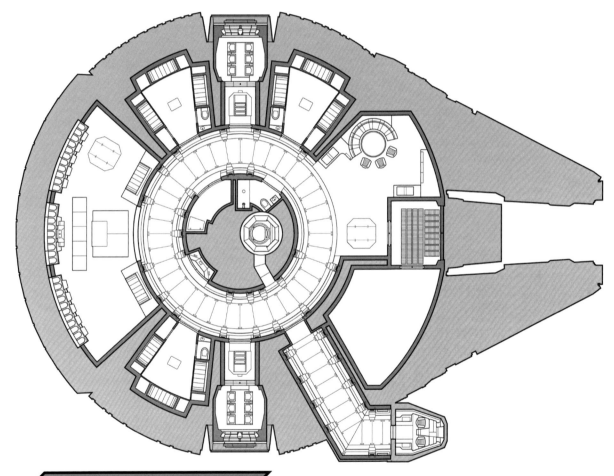

SPECIFICATIONS

CRAFT: YT-1300p
LENGTH: 34.75m
MAXIMUM SPEED (atmosphere): 800kph (500mph)
HYPERDRIVE: Class 2
HYPERDRIVE BACKUP: Class 12
SHIELDING: Equipped

NAVIGATION SYSTEM: Navicomputer
ARMAMENT: 1 standard laser cannon
CREW: 2
PASSENGERS: 9–15
CARGO: 25 metric tons
CONSUMABLES: 2 months
COST: 100,000 (25,000 used)

Exactly the opposite in concept of the YT-1300p, the YT-1300f configuration includes numerous cargo-hold modules but only the most basic accommodations for the crew. Industrial freight-loading arms and a tractor beam projector, more powerful than the units on the YT-1300p, are built into the inner edges of the mandibles to help move cargo directly into the freight loading room. Within the freight loading room, opposing hatches lead to the main hold and the fore cargo hold. Two additional cargo holds are located in the aft, on opposite sides of the engineering bay. The main

hold also includes the standard crew accommodations: two built-in bunks, which can be reconfigured as bunk beds, and a single refresher.

Port and starboard docking rings and boarding ramps allow easy access to a pair of passage tubes on either side of the YT-1300f. Secure hatches can transform both passage tubes into airlocks. Although Galactic law prohibits stowing cargo within passage tubes, and although the YT-1300f has ample room for cargo, records indicate that many pilots—when using the docking rings to connect with another ship or space station—transfer

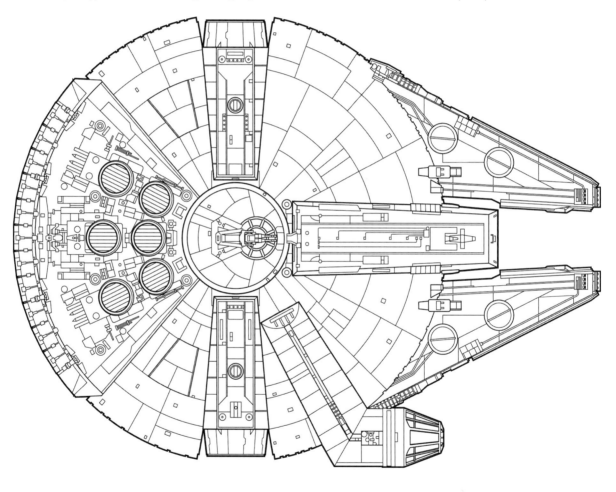

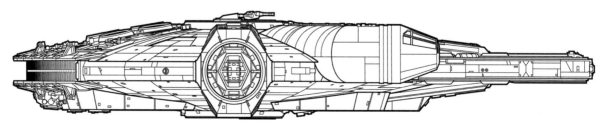

some cargo from the aft holds to a selected passage tube in advance so the cargo can be unloaded faster. In case of emergency, five single-occupant escape pods are located beneath floor hatches in the engineering bay. Beneath the engineering bay is a freight elevator that has a more powerful hydraulic system than its YT-1300p counterpart.

Both the YT-1300f and YT-1300p have a central passage tube that extends from the ventral to dorsal hull. A built-in ladder runs the length of this tube, and at each end of the tube is a transparisteel window.

Marketed as the 'observation deck', the tube's windows offer expansive views above and below the ship, and built-in gravity compensators allow travelers to move freely behind each window without any disorientation.

Although the YT-1300f's interior is more utilitarian than the YT-1300p, CEC acknowledges that passengers from different worlds have substantially different requirements for comfort. CEC offers a diverse range of modular and convertible furniture and bunks for all YT models. Obviously, travelers who don't require rest may have little or no need for bunks, and any additional space can be used for cargo.

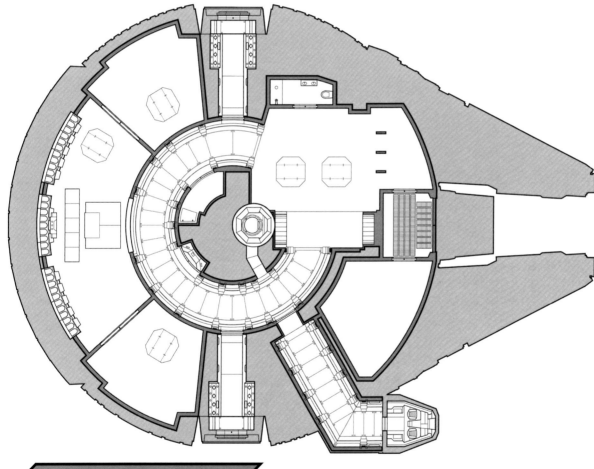

SPECIFICATIONS

CRAFT: YT-1300f
LENGTH: 34.75m
MAXIMUM SPEED (atmosphere): 800kph (500mph)
HYPERDRIVE: Class 2
HYPERDRIVE BACKUP: Class 12
SHIELDING: Equipped

NAVIGATION SYSTEM: Navicomputer
ARMAMENT: 1 standard laser cannon
CREW: 2
PASSENGERS: 6
CARGO: 100 metric tons
CONSUMABLES: 2 months
COST: 100,000 (25,000 used)

Both the YT-1300f and YT-1300p configurations were popular and sold well, but CEC soon grew wise to the fact that many customers were quick to customize the modules to create a better balance of space for cargo and passengers. CEC responded with a third configuration that was initially designated as the YT-1300fp, which represented the company's own interpretation of that sought-for balance of functionality.

The distinguishing features of the YT-1300fp were a single boarding ramp on the starboard side (because it provides quicker access to the cockpit corridor), a spacious main hold, a single cabin for the crew quarters, and a small lounge with a built-in galley. As with the YT-1300f, the boarding ramp, when raised, served as the floor of the passage tube that terminated at the starboard docking tube. The boarding ramp, industrial freight-loading arms, tractor beam projector, and freight elevator were the same as those found in the YT-1300f. For the crew quarters, the YT-1300fp utilized an existing module from the YT-1300p. New features included more powerful Girodyne sublight engines, stronger energy shields, a state-of-the-art Rubicon navicomputer, and a Quadex power core.

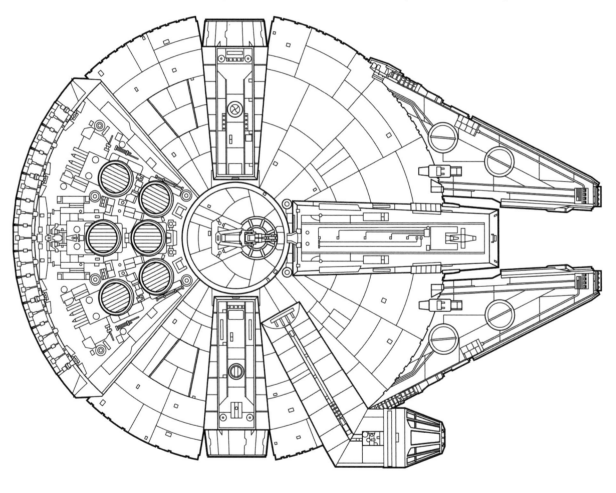

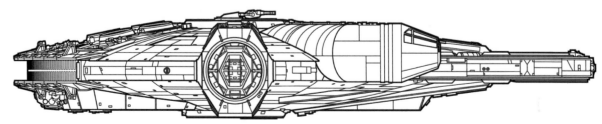

The new configuration proved a hit, and soon became so prevalent that it was commonly referred to as the 'stock' version of the YT-1300. Despite this common reference, and the fact that some CEC-authorized resellers offer 'stock' replacement parts, it should be noted that CEC never marketed a stock YT-1300, but rather promoted the fact that no two YT-1300 ships were exactly alike because each was outfitted to a customer's specific requirements before leaving the factory. The separate designations for the configurations eventually fell out of use, but some resellers and starshipwrights continue to refer to the YT-1300fp as a 'stock' YT-1300.

One negative aspect of the YT-1300fp was that Galactic Republic safety regulators and also the subsequent Imperial Navy questioned CEC's reasons for positioning a single Class-6 pod at the end of the port-side passage tube because an escape pod at the end of the opposite starboard tube would have provided more immediate access for anyone in the cockpit. CEC maintains that the Class-6 escape pod's position was more practical because most passengers were likely to congregate in the lounge or crew quarters.

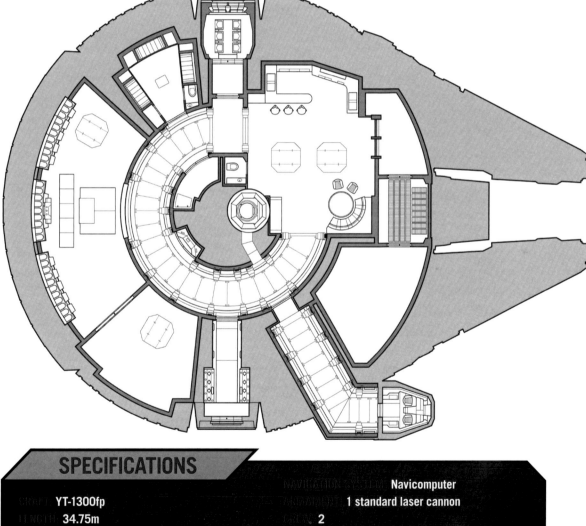

SPECIFICATIONS

CRAFT:	**YT-1300fp**		NAVIGATION SYSTEM:	**Navicomputer**
LENGTH:	**34.75m**		ARMAMENT:	**1 standard laser cannon**
MAXIMUM SPEED (atmosphere):	**800kph (500mph)**		CREW:	**2**
HYPERDRIVE:	**Class 2**		PASSENGERS:	**6**
HYPERDRIVE BACKUP:	**12**		CARGO:	**100 metric tons**
SHIELDING:	**Equipped**		CONSUMABLES:	**2 months**
			COST:	**100,000 (25,000 used)**

Although the majority of YT-1300 hull and cockpit configurations featured external starboard-mounted cockpits, CEC offered modular options for port-mounted cockpits, central-mounted cockpits (usually elevated directly above the gap between the mandibles), and cockpits that could be affixed to other positions on the hull. Some YT-1300s appear to have no obvious cockpit at all, as CEC also offered options for a completely armored ship with an 'embedded' cockpit, located under a heavily shielded hull, without any windows or viewports, a variation that depends heavily on visual sensors.

While some enthusiasts erroneously maintain that certain YT-1300 configurations were distinct models of the 'stock light freighter', even more vexing are contradictions about the ship's overall length. Not long after CEC began production of the YT-1300, the model's keel length was improperly recorded on official classification documents, an error in specification that was distributed to spaceports all over the galaxy. Some have attributed the gaffe to a malfunctioning secretarial droid who allegedly served either CEC or the Bureau of Ships and Services (BoSS), while others have blamed it on a policy of misinformation within the highly competitive shipbuilding industry. A few industry insiders purported that the ship's *estimated* length was filed with the BoSS before the forward mandibles had been incorporated into the design. Spaceport officials and frustrated pilots were among the first to catch on to the numerical discrepancy because YT-1300s were frequently assigned to docking bays that were too small to accommodate their actual bulk.

Yet another problem turned up when starship mechanics realized that CEC did not authorize the publication of many of the YT-1300 design documents that remain in circulation, and which feature vastly different internal layouts than can be found in existing ships. Some of these documents were based on legitimate alternate designs offered by CEC to buyers seeking customization, but most of these designs were for configurations that were never produced. Evidently, early in the design phase several different sets of prototype deck plans and scale models were stolen from a CEC shipyard office. These materials became widely available, and because they bear official CEC seals the designs are still frequently mistaken as schematics for actual starships.

As a public service, CEC has provided the following diagrams to distinguish the better-known YT-1300 transport variants from unauthorized replicas.

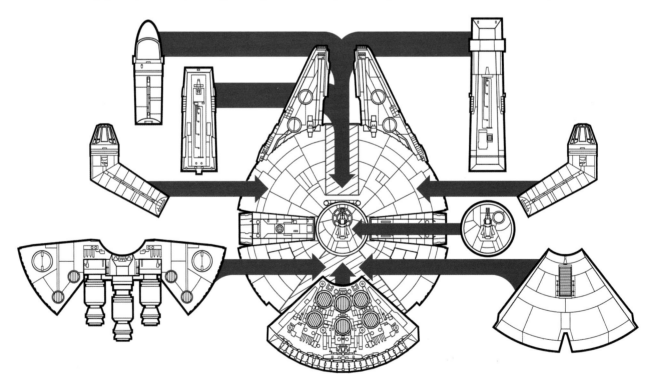

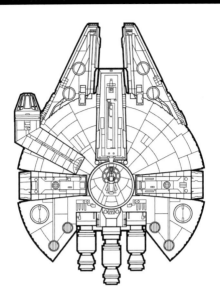 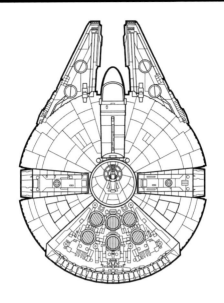 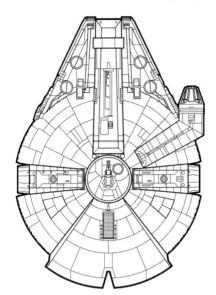

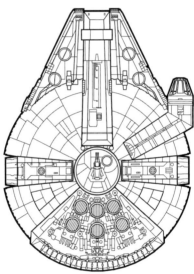 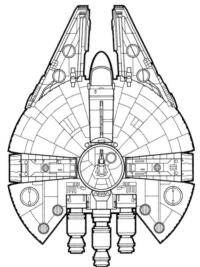 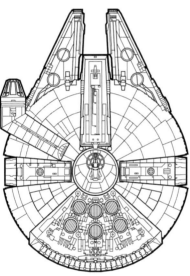

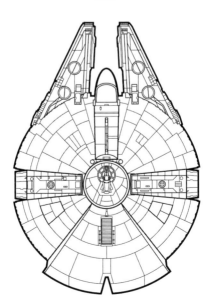 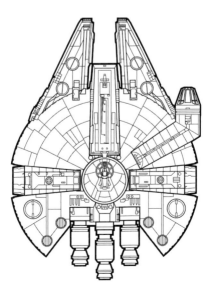 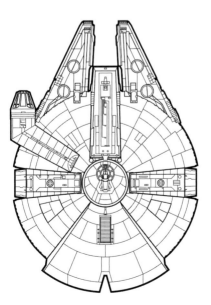

Durable hull armor and upgraded shield projectors are standard options for the YT-1300. The armor's weight sacrifices speed, reduces the payload, and impedes maneuverability, but enables the YT-1300 to operate in extremely harsh environments. Five landing gear emplacements are required to accommodate the additional weight.

Because the fully armored YT is without transparisteel windows, a traditional cockpit is replaced by a control station concealed within the ship. Heavy-duty sensor emplacements transmit data and visual displays of surrounding space to the armored ship's crew. The viewports in the observation decks are replaced with opaque optical sensor domes, which are adjustable for different light spectrums such as infrared and ultraviolet. Cannon turrets are equipped with large viewscreens that present clear pictures of surrounding areas and targets.

ARMORED HULL

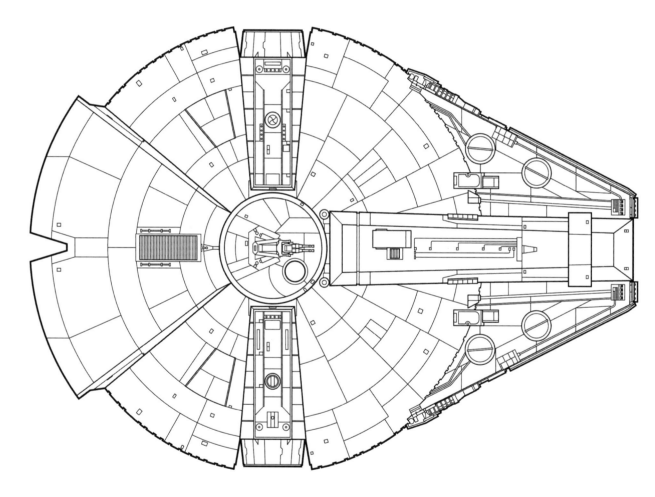

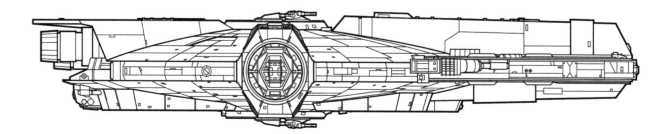

Unlike the early models in the YT-series, which had two or three cylindrical engines, the YT-1300 is equipped with what has come to be known as a 'wide bar' engine. The wide bar generates greater thrust and has multiple steering flaps that allow unprecedented maneuverability for a YT, but because some pilots were unable or unwilling to adapt to the more controlled engine system, CEC offered cylindrical engines as an alternative.

Another option was a central-oriented cockpit, similar to the YT-1000, which provides a wider field of view. For this configuration, CEC recommends a ventral gun turret mount or an elevated dorsal mount that allows forward-firing clearance over the cockpit and prevents carbon scoring to the canopy's upper windows. Interestingly, most pilots who preferred cylindrical engines on the YT-1300 also preferred a central-mounted cockpit.

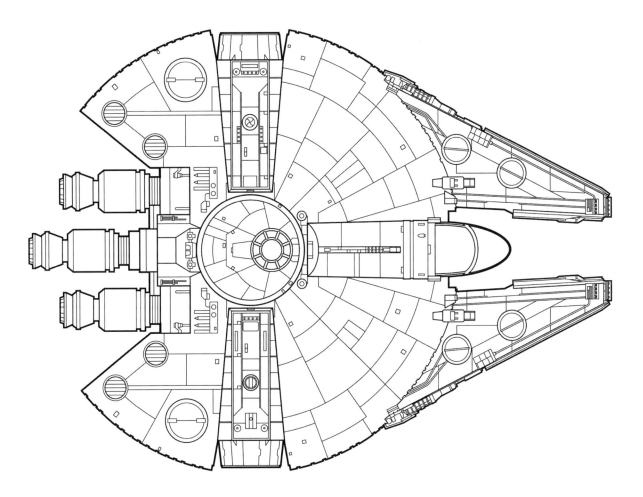

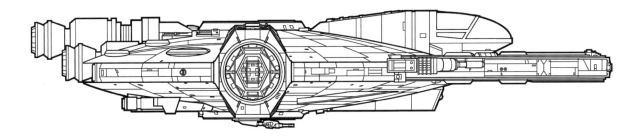

For YT-1300 pilots who require additional cargo space, CEC offers a range of cargo pods that mount to the ship's exterior. The most popular cargo-pod system consists of five sturdy, utilitarian shells that encircle more than half of the ship's dorsal hull, and nearly double the overall cargo capacity. The pods can be installed or removed via tractor beams, and are easily accessed from above, Although each standard pod is vacuum-sealed, they are not designed or engineered to transport most life forms.

Before adding cargo pods, pilots should determine whether their existing engine power is sufficient to accommodate a heavier payload. Also, shields, sensors and weapons emplacements may need to be relocated to the ventral hull to make room for the pods. While the cargo pods require time to load and unload, they are time and cost effective in that they are considerably less expensive than maintaining a second ship.

CARGO PODS

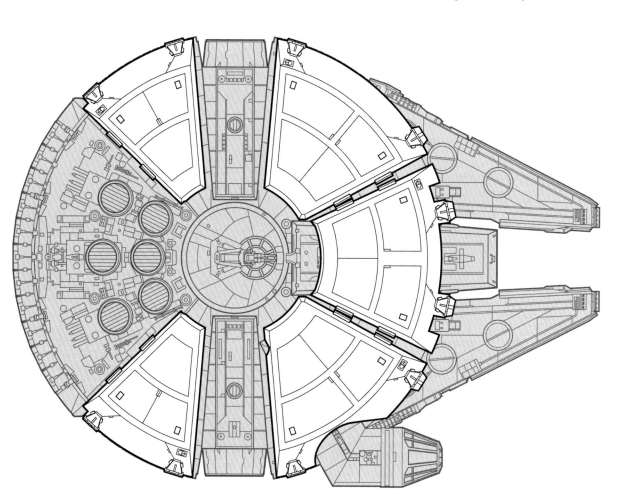

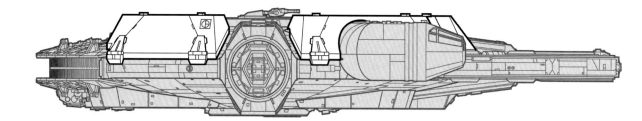

The YT-1300 can be outfitted with either rigid or inflatable pontoons for water landings. Rigid pontoons are preferred by commercial pilots with dedicated routes between water worlds, while inflatable pontoons appeal more to safety-minded pilots. Inflatable pontoons can be inflated with either pressurized gas from dedicated tanks or by modifying the 'landing jets' to divert atmospheric or pressurized gas into the pontoons. Four rectangular pontoons frame the ship's landing gear while four spherical pontoons elevate the mandibles.

Although pontoons are a practical way to keep a spaceship afloat, a properly maintained YT-1300 is capable of making an emergency water landing, staying afloat, and launching from the water. However, CEC stresses that all hatches should be properly secured before and during any water landings to prevent flooding that could cause the ship to sink.

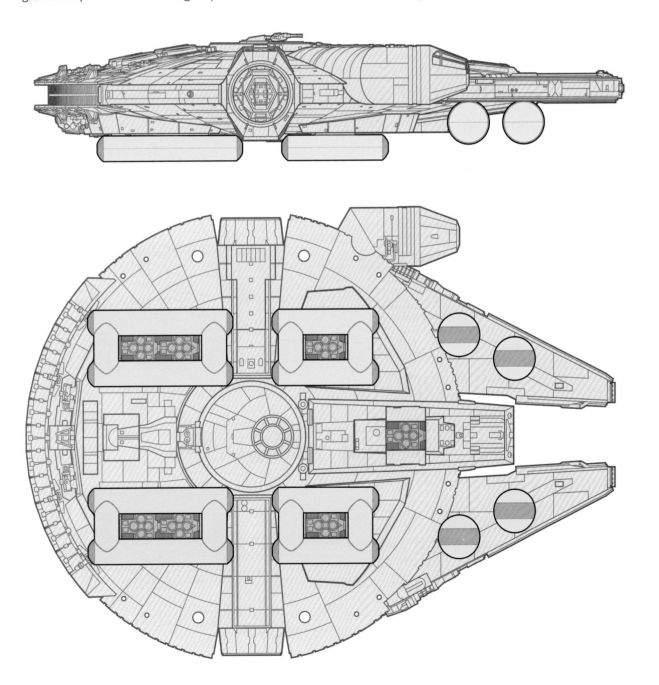

F-LER

A truly rare vehicle, the single-pilot F-LER—an acronym for 'freight-loading external rover'—was briefly manufactured by Corellian Engineering Corporation and used in CEC orbital assembly facilities, but was never sold commercially. The vehicle was inspired by a mini-tug, used to transfer unsold YT-1200 and YT-1210 ships to a facility where they would be upgraded into 'new' YT-1250 models; when CEC ship-designer Tem Riffle saw the mini-tug leading a YT-1200 across space, he suddenly envisioned a small cargo-handler that could fit between the mandibles of a YT-1300, directly in front of the YT-1300's freight-loading room.

CEC executives loved Riffle's proposal for a modular cargo-handler, capable of traveling in either space or atmospheres, as it not only presented a new option for consumers but also seemed to serve a practical purpose: the compact F-LER would enable YT-1300 pilots to pick up or deliver freight to locations that were inaccessible to their freighters. Most designers agreed that the cargo-hauler added a sleeker look to the YT's overall profile. CEC's marketing department predicted YT-1300 owners would be eager to 'fill the gap' between the mandibles with an F-LER. After successfully testing a prototype, CEC began production of a limited run, and the marketing department prepared a survey that was

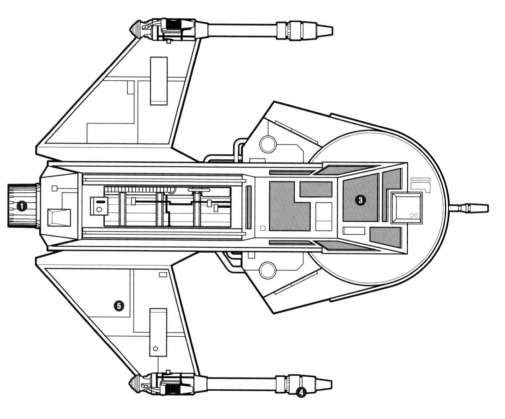

❶ Thruster
❷ Docking hatch
❸ Cockpit canopy
❹ Laser cannon (2, optional)
❺ Stabilizer (2)
❻ Harpoon gun and tow cable

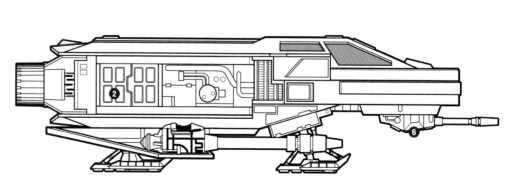

transmitted to 500 commercial pilots who had recently purchased YT-1300s.

Barely a week into production, the marketing department collated the survey results and discovered that they had grossly overestimated interest in the F-LER. In fact, most pilots were simply against the idea of sticking a vehicle between the mandibles. As one pilot noted, 'The YT-1300 already has freight-loading arms and a tractor beam between the mandibles. When I touch down at most spaceports, it's easy enough to load and unload freight as is. The F-LER might be occasionally useful, but I need to move freight in or out of the freight-loading room quickly, and the F-LER would just be in the way. I'd have to remove it first, and then I'd have to put it back before lift-off. In other words, a waste of time.' Another pilot was more blunt: 'To use the F-LER, I'd have to get out of my YT-1300. Who wants that?'

CEC saved a hundred F-LERs as tugs and scrapped the rest. Eventually a few made their way to the open market; one well-known modified version was armed with CEC Ap/11 dual laser cannons, but these were not standard. Today, a refurbished F-LER is worth more than a vintage 'stock' YT-1300.

MINI-FIGHTER

Despite the F-LER's lack of success, the research and development that went into the F-LER soon found its way into a CEC-manufactured single-pilot exploration craft, designated the YT-XC, which was also built specifically for the YT-1300. Unlike the F-LER, the YT-XC was housed *within* the YT-1300, hidden behind a modular hatch that appeared to be either the port or starboard 'docking ring'. Although the addition of a YT-XC meant the loss of one docking ring, CEC banked on the idea that a concealed ship would have great appeal to many customers. The response was tremendous. In deference to concerns expressed by Imperial Customs, CEC marketed the YT-XC to relief organizations, licensed industrial prospectors, and scientific foundations. However, the YT-XC became most popular with pirates and smugglers, who did not hesitate to add blaster cannons and concussion missile launchers that transformed the craft into a miniature starfighter. Subsequently the YT-XC became popularly known as a 'mini-fighter'.

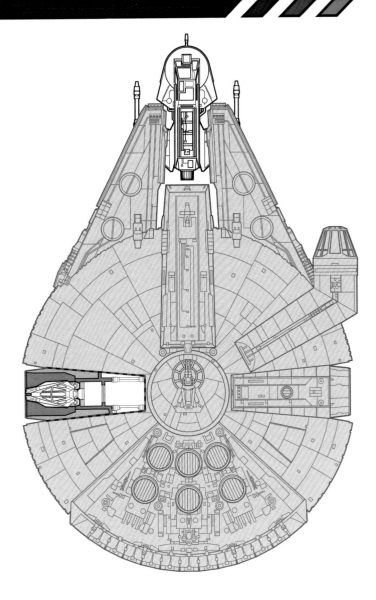

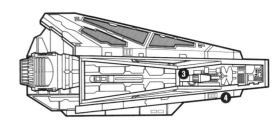

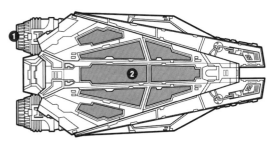

1. **Thrusters**
2. **Cockpit canopy**
3. **Blaster cannons (2)**
4. **Weapon emplacement**

Prior to the debut of the YT-1300, CEC released the YT-1200 and YT-1210, both of which sported a side-mounted cockpit, a long sensor-laden boom that extended out over the fore hull, and a total of ten attachment points for optional add-ons. The two ships were distinguished by the number of their respective thrusters: the YT-1200 had two thrusters, and the YT-1210 had three. Although CEC offered numerous modular options, customers preferred the YT-1000 —and after the incredibly popular YT-1300 was released, CEC found themselves stuck with a huge back stock of unsold and largely unwanted YT-1200 and YT-1210 freighters.

In an effort to generate revenue from the unsold YT-1200 and YT-1210, CEC upgraded their remaining stock and remarketed them as a 'new' product, which they designated the YT-1250. CEC raised more money by subsequently sub-licensing the YT-1200's manufacturing plans to another manufacturer, Nova-Drive. Nova-Drive remodeled the YT-1200 and marketed it as the 3-Z light freighter.

The YT-1250 represented an unusual move on the part of CEC, as they normally left all upgrades and modifications to starship purchasers. CEC added more powerful engines, heavier weapons, and a basic set of defensive shields, all in an effort to make the YT-1250 more desirable. As a result, the YT-1250 is actually more durable than the YT-1300. However, the upgrades left the YT-1250 with 20% less cargo capacity than a stock YT-1210, and only six

YT-1200

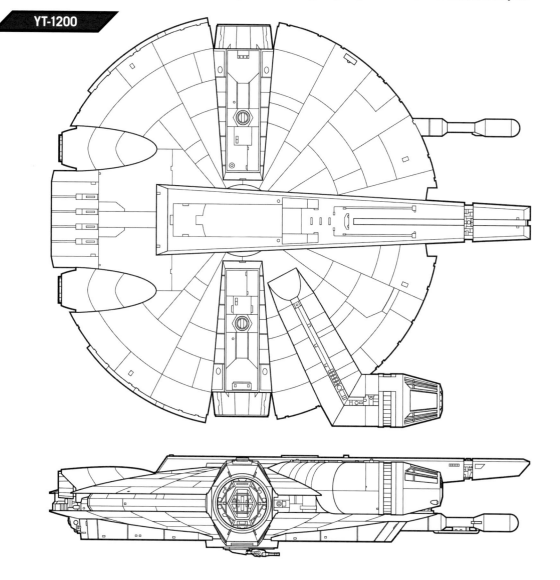

attachment points instead of the ten available on most YT-series freighters.

CEC marketed the YT-1250 as appropriate for light defense duties, cargo duties in more hazardous regions of space, and as armed merchant ships to protect freighter convoys. Although the boom carried enhanced sensors that allowed pilots to travel more easily through bad-visibility areas, such as nebular clouds or densely gaseous planetary atmospheres, sales were sluggish because of the upgraded ship's increased cost and reduced cargo capacity. CEC eventually sold the remaining stock to small, peaceful systems and militant trade guilds. Many YT-1250s remain in operation, and are popular with couriers, bounty hunters, smugglers, and pirates.

SPECIFICATIONS

CRAFT:	YT-1250
LENGTH:	32.25m
MAXIMUM SPEED (atmosphere):	800kph (500mph)
HYPERDRIVE:	Class 2
HYPERDRIVE BACKUP:	Class 16
SHIELDING:	Equipped
NAVIGATION SYSTEM:	Navicomputer
ARMAMENT:	1 double laser cannon
CREW:	2
PASSENGERS:	5
CARGO:	80 metric tons
CONSUMABLES:	3 months
COST:	120,000 (30,000 used)

YT-1250

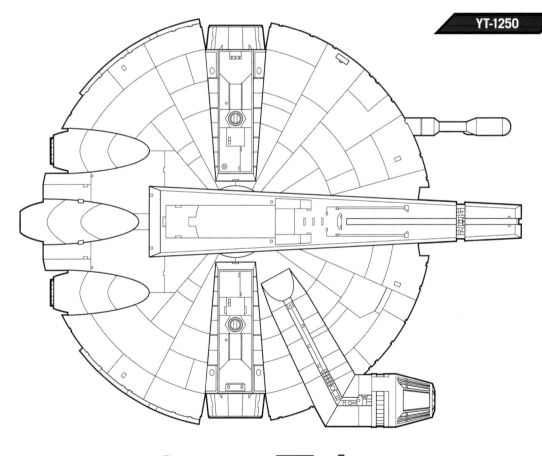

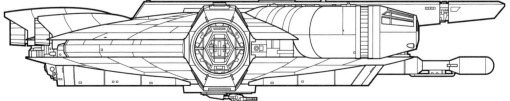

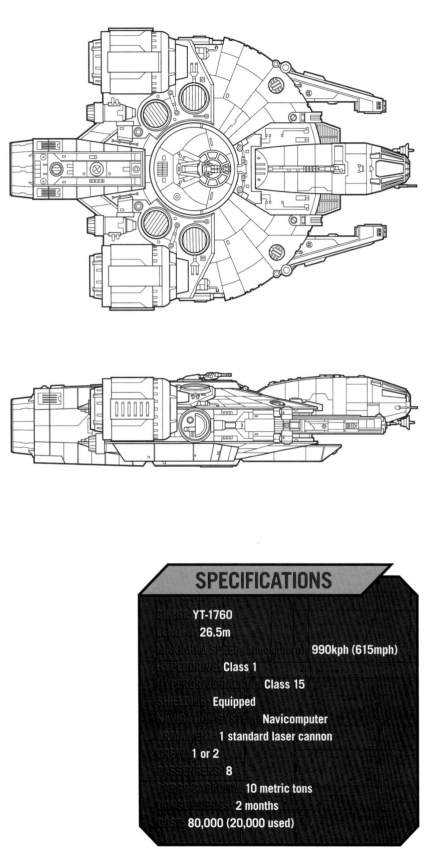

Released 32 years before the Battle of Yavin, the YT-1760 Small Transport was marketed as a transport and shuttle ship. It was specifically designed to overcome some of the problems found to be common with older YT models, such as a lack of power in the sublight drives, poor maneuverability, and slow hyperdrive speed. Unfortunately, the upgrades came at the expense of durability and cargo capacity. Even worse, its less sturdy design usually resulted in higher maintenance costs. By the time of the Rebellion era, the most likely place to find an original YT-1760 was in a scrapyard.

However, even the most problematic YT models have their enthusiasts, and the YT-1760 is no exception. The central cockpit allows for better visibility than YT models with side-mounted cockpits, and most pilots agree that the YT-1760 is an exceptionally maneuverable transport. The maneuverability is due almost entirely to the design and strategic orientation of the bulked-up engines and secondary thrusters, which enable a stock YT-1760 to execute sharper turns, tighter rolls, and fly 190km (119mph) faster than a standard YT-1300. Also, like all YT-series ships, the YT-1760 is highly modifiable, and long-time owners know all the most economical upgrades.

A common modification is to take some of the limited cargo space and use it to install more powerful shield generators, which greatly increase the ship's survivability. Although the stock YT-1760 initially came without armaments, CEC responded to customer complaints by adding a standard laser cannon. Two turret mounts—similar to those found on the YT-1300—can readily accommodate larger commercial laser cannons. For the owner who wants some degree of luxury, the YT-1760's standard small bunks can be easily removed and replaced with more comfortable modular staterooms.

Obviously, the YT-1760's relatively small cargo space never encouraged interest from larger trade guilds and transport companies, but the YT-1760 remains popular with independent traders, smugglers, and pirates.

SPECIFICATIONS

CRAFT:	YT-1760
LENGTH:	26.5m
MAXIMUM SPEED (atmosphere):	990kph (615mph)
HYPERDRIVE:	Class 1
HYPERDRIVE BACKUP:	Class 15
SHIELDING:	Equipped
NAVIGATION SYSTEM:	Navicomputer
ARMAMENT:	1 standard laser cannon
CREW:	1 or 2
PASSENGERS:	8
CARGO CAPACITY:	10 metric tons
CONSUMABLES:	2 months
COST:	80,000 (20,000 used)

The YT-1930 was not an entirely new design, but one of the more significant variants of the YT-1300. The YT-1930's cockpit is centrally located atop the ship, positioned directly above and between the forward mandibles. The ship has upgraded shield generators, hull, and sublight drives. Unlike the 'stock' YT-1300, which was equipped with a light laser cannon, the YT-1930 came armed with a turret-mounted medium laser cannon in the area typically designated for a YT observation deck's dorsal window.

The most distinguishing features of the YT-1930 are the flared, wedge-shaped sections that extend from the aft. When the YT-1930 debuted, those who were unfamiliar with the design assumed that the flared sections were modular add-ons for transporting cargo, but these sections—which are in fact cargo areas— are fully integrated parts of the ship. Compared with other YT models, the YT-1930 has twice as much or more cargo capacity, and cargo could be easily loaded and unloaded through hatches on the aft sections. The aft sections also serve as full-ship stabilizers and 'natural' brakes in atmospheric flights. The consensus among most pilots was that the YT-1930 offered a more stable ride than any previous YT, and a number of shipping companies embraced the ship for the simple reason that it made economic sense: a single YT-1930 cost less than two YT-1300s, but could carry as much cargo.

However, not everyone was impressed with the YT-1930's overall design. Although the cockpit's central-forward location offers a wider view than the side-mounted cockpits on YT-1300s, it raised questions about the practicality of the forward mandibles. While the YT-1930's mandibles do contain many necessary components, they are without built-in freight-loading arms because the cockpit blocks the traditional YT loading area. Also, the flared aft sections limit the ship's docking capability. Where a YT-1300 can brace its docking rings up against a broad, flat expanse, the YT-1930 cannot, and also requires a larger docking bay.

Less than a thousand YT-1930s were produced, as the ship's design innovations were quickly implemented into its successor, the YT-2000, which effectively rendered the YT-1930 obsolete.

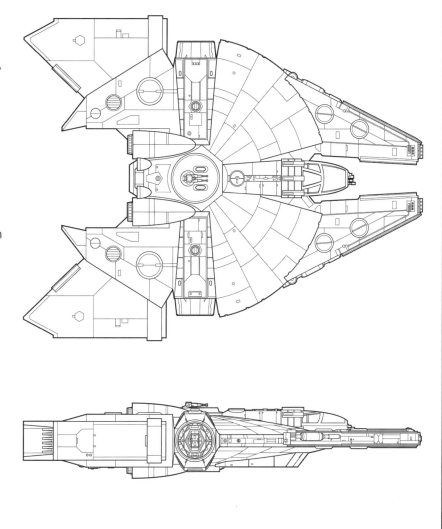

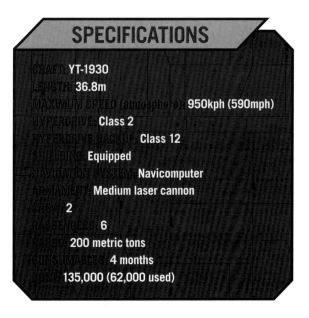

SPECIFICATIONS

CRAFT:	YT-1930
LENGTH:	36.8m
MAXIMUM SPEED (atmosphere):	950kph (590mph)
HYPERDRIVE:	Class 2
HYPERDRIVE BACKUP:	Class 12
SHIELDING:	Equipped
NAVIGATION SYSTEM:	Navicomputer
ARMAMENT:	Medium laser cannon
CREW:	2
PASSENGERS:	6
CARGO:	200 metric tons
CONSUMABLES:	4 months
COST:	135,000 (62,000 used)

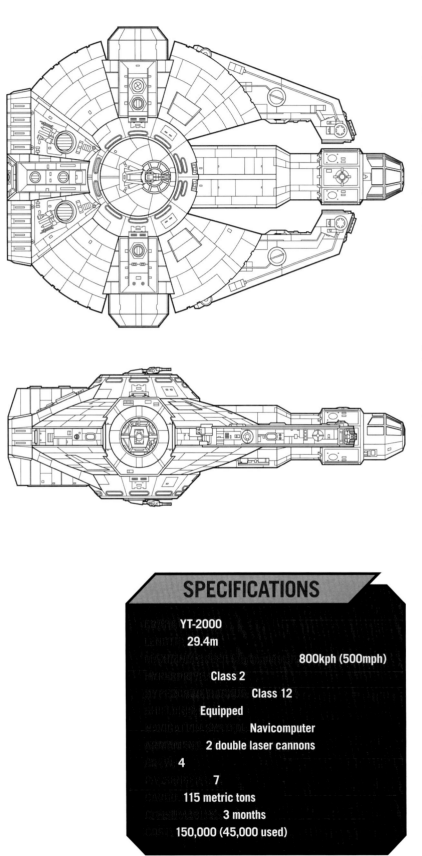

Conceived as a straight improvement on the YT-1300, the YT-2000 was a new design, built from the ground up, but borrowed successful design concepts from other YT models. Like the YT-1300, the YT-2000 has a fairly symmetrical layout, but can carry 15 metric tons more cargo than the standard YT-1300. The YT-2000 was designed for the civilian market during the period that the Rebel Alliance rose up against the Galactic Empire, and boasted heavier standard shields and weapons than most civilian freighters. Although CEC maintained these upgrades were a necessary precaution against pirates who had become more daring during the turbulent Rebellion, many Imperial officials regarded CEC's 'civilian' market with suspicion.

While the YT-2000's centrally positioned cockpit is evocative of the YT-1930, the YT-2000's cockpit juts out beyond the mandibles for an unobstructed view unprecedented in previous models. The cockpit also represented one of CEC's most dramatic design innovations for the YT series, as a standard option for the YT-2000 was a cockpit module that doubled as an emergency lifeboat, engineered to break away from the ship in an emergency. CEC knew this would appeal not only to safety-minded crews who otherwise would have had to leave the cockpit in order to evacuate the freighter by either an escape pod or ancillary vehicle. Optional add-ons equipped the lifeboat-cockpit with a Class 12 hyperdrive.

Unfortunately, CEC was victimized by extensive corporate espionage, and the YT-2000's early design specifications were leaked to competing shipyards. The leak prompted CEC to put the YT-2000 into production before the design and ship's systems could be thoroughly tested. Not surprisingly, the result was a ship regarded as 'somewhat touchier' than the more reliable YT designs, but the YT-2000 proved immediately popular with owners for its admirable qualities: extensive cargo capacity, strong defensive systems, amazing maneuverability for a ship its size, and many opportunities for modifications. Despite good sales, the YT-2000 was discontinued early when CEC unveiled the subsequent YT-2400, which had not been compromised by espionage or rushed production.

SPECIFICATIONS

CRAFT	YT-2000
LENGTH	29.4m
MAXIMUM SPEED (ATMOSPHERE)	800kph (500mph)
HYPERDRIVE	Class 2
HYPERDRIVE (BACKUP)	Class 12
SHIELDING	Equipped
NAVIGATION SYSTEM	Navicomputer
ARMAMENT	2 double laser cannons
CREW	4
PASSENGERS	7
CARGO	115 metric tons
CONSUMABLES	3 months
COST	150,000 (45,000 used)

Designed by CEC as a 'stock cargo hauler', the YT-2400 light freighter has reinforced bulkhead frames and double-armored exterior hull plating, and was originally intended for use in the more competitive and hazardous regions of the Outer Rim Territories. The YT-2400 maintains the trademark saucer-shaped hull of most YT-series ships, but is distinguished by an elongated, cylindrical cockpit module connected to the hull by two starboard bracing arms.

CEC promotes the YT-2400 as offering most of the best features of the YT-1300 in a more maneuverable design, one that's easily operated by a single pilot. The YT-2400 uses many of the same parts as the YT-1300 and other CEC ships, but incorporates the parts in a streamlined and somewhat more compact frame. Despite its size, the stock YT-2400 can actually carry more cargo than the stock YT-1300.

Unlike the YT-1300, the YT-2400 comes with strong shields as standard equipment and has weapon hardpoints built in. Standard weapons include two laser cannons, dorsal and ventral, mounted on Corellian 1D servo turrets. A total of 13 weapon emplacement points are built into the design, with six used in the ship's stock configuration, leaving seven free for easy modification. The YT-2400's power core has nearly twice the output of other YT models, allowing for oversized engines and additional modifications to utilize the extra energy.

The cockpit module has an access tube running aft to the primary escape pod, which is built for six. Crew quarters and living areas, located in the bracing arms, are not as spacious as other YT models, but much more room has been given over for modifications. A secondary escape pod is located in the saucer hull cargo area, directly opposite the primary escape craft.

By the time CEC released the YT-2000 and the YT-2400, their customer base had come to broadly accept and generally prefer the wide bar engine popularized by the YT-1300. CEC did not offer cylindrical engines as standard options for either the YT-2000 or YT-2400, but CEC-authorized modification kits are available to customers who wish to customize their vessels for cylindrical engines.

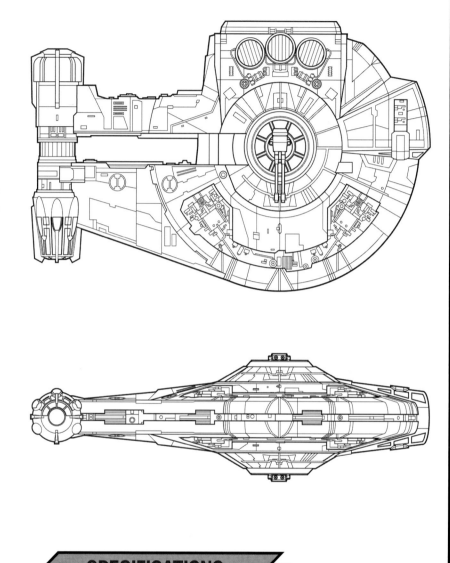

SPECIFICATIONS

CRAFT:	YT-2400		
LENGTH:	18.65m	WIDTH:	28.5m
MAXIMUM SPEED (atmosphere):			800kph (500mph)
HYPERDRIVE:	Class 2		
HYPERDRIVE BACKUP:		Class 12	
SHIELDING:	Equipped		
NAVIGATION SYSTEM:		Navicomputer	
ARMAMENT:		2 turret-mounted dual laser cannons	
CREW:	3		
PASSENGERS:	6		
CARGO:	150 metric tons		
CONSUMABLES:		2 months	
COST:	130,000 (32,000 used)		

THE MILLENNIUM FALCON

Imperial alert transmitted after the Battle of Yavin

The Imperial Navy is searching for a CEC YT-1300 light freighter named the *Millennium Falcon*. According to data gathered from Mos Eisley Spaceport on the planet Tatooine, the *Millennium Falcon* is owned and operated by a Corellian smuggler and former Imperial pilot, Han Solo, and his partner Chewbacca, a Wookiee. The *Millennium Falcon* appears unremarkable but has been illegally modified for increased shield power and speed, and carries military-grade weapons. Imperial authorities most recently sighted the ship at Monastery and Ord Mantell.

Han Solo and Chewbacca are associates of the Rebel Alliance, and are wanted for the following crimes against the Empire:

- Liberation of a known criminal, Princess Leia Organa of Alderaan
- Direct involvement in armed revolt against the Empire
- High treason
- Espionage
- Conspiracy
- Destruction of Imperial property

Han Solo and Chewbacca are considered extremely dangerous. The Empire is offering a bounty of 300,000 credits for their capture. The bounty is for live capture only. The Empire will not be held responsible for any injuries or property loss arising from the attempted apprehension of these notorious criminals. Anyone with information about the whereabouts of the *Millennium Falcon* and her crew should contact the nearest branch of the Imperial Intelligence Office.

Imperial Security image-capture of the *Millennium Falcon* near the Starshipyards of Fondor.

Although numerous details of the *Millennium Falcon's* history may have been lost to time, the vessel's serial number, YT 492727ZED, remains etched into various sections of her original framework. According to Corellian Engineering Corporation (CEC) records, YT 492727ZED was constructed as a YT-1300 freighter at CEC Orbital Assembly Facility 7 less than a year after the YT-1300 series went into production, 60 years before the Battle of Yavin.

Like most of the YT-1300 freighters leaving Orbital Assembly Facility 7, YT 492727ZED had a waiting buyer: Corell Industries (CI) Limited, a shipping company that had, at the time, a fleet of more than 8,000 vessels. CI Limited ferried goods to the Five Brothers—the collective name of the Corellian worlds Corellia, Drall, Talus, Tralus, and Selonia—and also to the incredibly ancient and enormous space station known as Centerpoint Station.

Under CI Limited's ownership, YT 492727ZED had at least three different names over the course of 12 years, including *Corell's Pride*, *Fickle Flyer*, and *Meetyl's Misery*. Entries from the freighter's built-in flight recorder reveal varying accounts of the ship's performance. Interestingly, almost all the entries include terms normally used to describe the personality of a sentient being. Many pilots commented on the freighter's remarkable speed and maneuverability, while others found the ship quirky and notoriously unreliable.

Unfortunately for CI Limited, the monopolistic Trade Federation began taking control of the routes between the Five Brothers, and the Republic Senate did nothing to help. Losing profits, CI Limited was forced to sell its ships at absurdly low prices before the company fell into bankruptcy and went out of business.

YT 492727ZED was among the last ships to be sold by CI Limited, and was purchased by Kal and Dova Brigger, a brother and sister team of freelance traders from the Corellia system. The Briggers renamed the ship *Hardwired*, and briefly moved freight between the Five Brothers, essentially resuming certain runs previously established by CI Limited. Contemporaneous records suggest the Briggers must have invested all their profits in upgrading their freighter's hyperdrive, for they soon expanded operations to neighboring star systems and then to the Core. HoloNet entries indicate that the *Hardwired's* standard cargo changed from

→ The YT-1300 *Stellar Envoy*—later renamed the *Millennium Falcon*—approaching the Senate Building on Coruscant.

consumer goods to weapons and contraband.

According to other HoloNet entries, the Briggers became associated with the Smugglers' Confederacy of the Cularin system, and the organization's leader, the Oblee crime lord Nirama, helped them finance further upgrades in exchange for their pledge to refrain from conducting business with slavers. The association ended a standard year later, when the Briggers reneged, and Nirama placed a bounty on their heads. A bounty hunter captured Dova Brigger, and Nirama had Dova executed.

Kal Brigger fled, renamed the YT *Wayward Son*, and changed its registry to Fondor before he proceeded to Thyferra. He became involved with Iaco Stark's Commercial Combine, a criminal collective that worked the Rimma Trade Route. Following an attack by Republic Forces, Kal wound up in an abandoned spice mine on Troiken, where he was eaten alive by carnivorous insects.

HoloNet records reveal the next mention of the *Wayward Son* was 15 years after Kal Brigger's death, when the ship became the property of the Republic Group, an obscure and possibly secret organization linked to holding companies on Coruscant, Alderaan, and Corellia. Under the Republic Group's ownership, the YT-1300 was registered to Ralltiir, renamed *Stellar Envoy*, and was piloted by Tobb Jadak, a former prizewinning swoop racer. During the Battle of Coruscant, the *Stellar Envoy* was cleared to land at the Senate Building, and left Coruscant shortly afterward. The ship proceeded to Nar Shaddaa, where she collided with the departing bulk freighter *Jendirian Valley III*. Jadak and his co-pilot Reeze Duurmun may have evacuated in an escape pod, but their bodies were never found. Despite severe damage, the *Stellar Envoy* was restored. Serial numbers indicate that the ship's cockpit, mandibles, and main hold were salvaged from a YT-1300p that had collided with an asteroid near Nal Hutta.

While evidence of other modifications suggest YT 492727ZED changed ownership more than once after the Clone Wars, records provide mostly sketchy details. But by the time a rogue named Lando Calrissian was introduced to the ship, she was named the *Millennium Falcon*.

⬆ **Painted in the colors of the Republic Group, the *Stellar Envoy* leaves Coruscant during the Clone Wars.**

⬇ **Jabba the Hutt and his men beside the *Millennium Falcon* in Docking Bay 94 in Mos Eisley Spaceport on Tatooine.**

STARBOARD

DORSAL

VENTRAL

MILLENNIUM FALCON: VIEWS

FORWARD

AFT

SPECIFICATIONS

CURRENT DESIGNATION: Millennium Falcon
MANUFACTURER: Corellian Engineering Corporation
MAKE: Corellian YT-1300f light freighter (modified)
SERIAL NUMBER: YT 492727ZED
LENGTH: 34.37m
MAXIMUM SPEED (atmosphere): 1,050kph (650mph)
HYPERDRIVE: Class 0.5
BACKUP HYPERDRIVE: Class 10
ENGINES: Quadex power core, powering Isu-Sim SSP05 hyperdrive generator (heavily modified); 2 Girodyne SRB42 sublight engines (heavily modified)

SHIELDING: Military-grade deflector shield generators
NAVIGATION: Rubicon navicomputer with Microaxial HyD modular navicomputer backup (modified)
ARMAMENT: 2 CEC AG-2G quad laser cannons, 2 Arakyd ST2 concussion missile tubes, 1 BlasTech Ax-108 'Ground Buzzer' blaster cannon
CREW: 2 (minimum)
PASSENGERS: 6
CARGO: 100 metric tons
CONSUMABLES: 2 months
COST: Not available for sale

DORSAL 3/4

VENTRAL 3/4

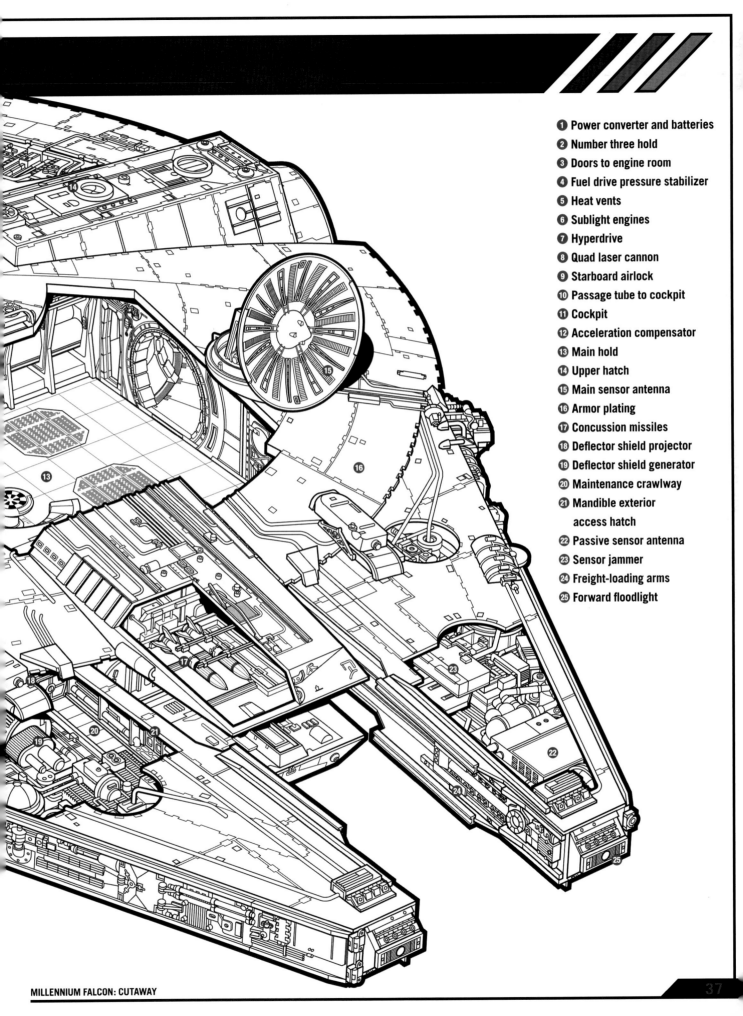

1. Power converter and batteries
2. Number three hold
3. Doors to engine room
4. Fuel drive pressure stabilizer
5. Heat vents
6. Sublight engines
7. Hyperdrive
8. Quad laser cannon
9. Starboard airlock
10. Passage tube to cockpit
11. Cockpit
12. Acceleration compensator
13. Main hold
14. Upper hatch
15. Main sensor antenna
16. Armor plating
17. Concussion missiles
18. Deflector shield projector
19. Deflector shield generator
20. Maintenance crawlway
21. Mandible exterior access hatch
22. Passive sensor antenna
23. Sensor jammer
24. Freight-loading arms
25. Forward floodlight

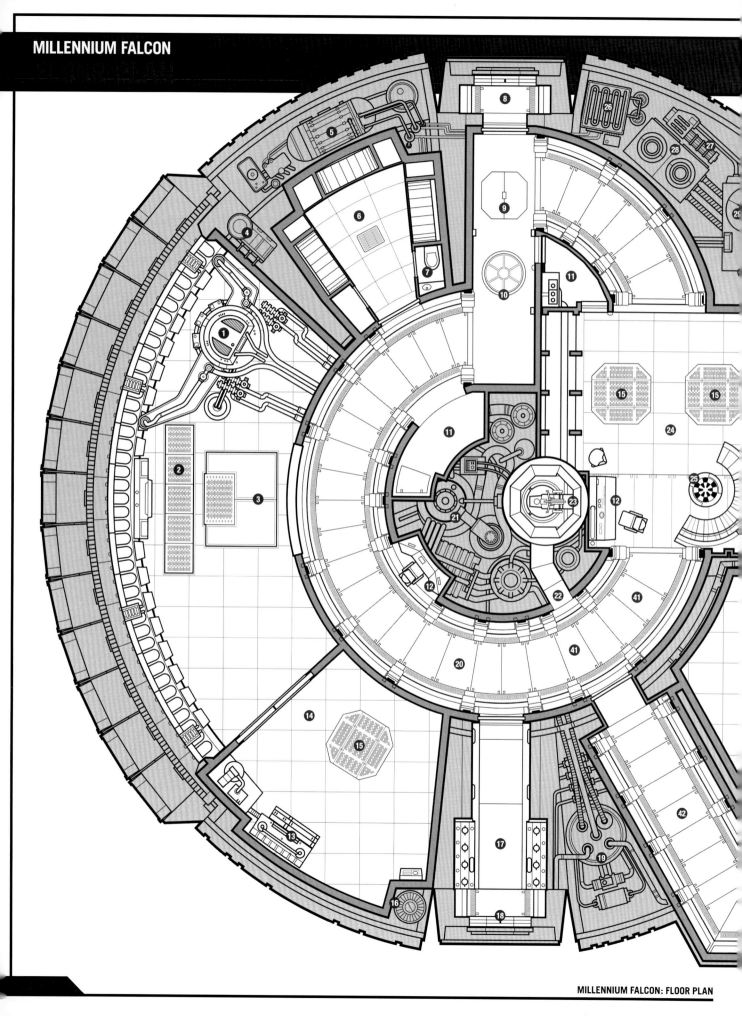

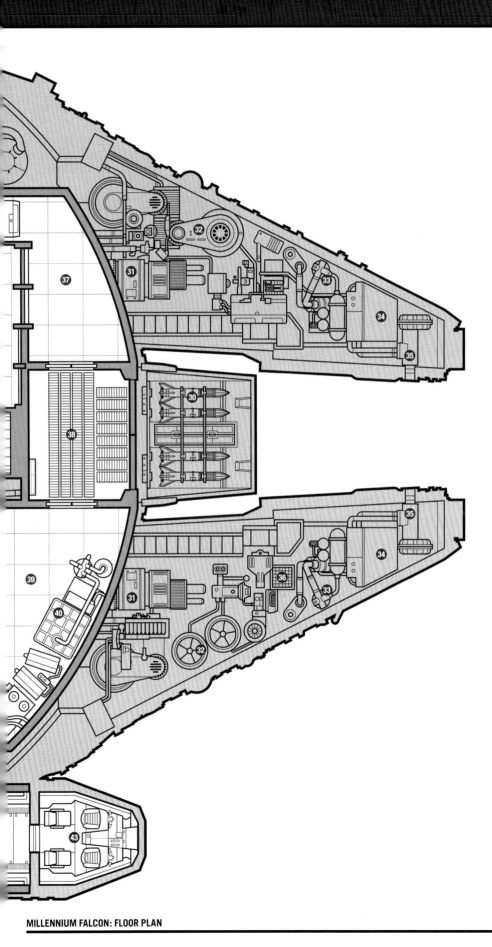

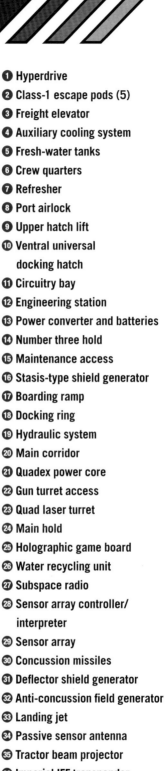

1. Hyperdrive
2. Class-1 escape pods (5)
3. Freight elevator
4. Auxiliary cooling system
5. Fresh-water tanks
6. Crew quarters
7. Refresher
8. Port airlock
9. Upper hatch lift
10. Ventral universal docking hatch
11. Circuitry bay
12. Engineering station
13. Power converter and batteries
14. Number three hold
15. Maintenance access
16. Stasis-type shield generator
17. Boarding ramp
18. Docking ring
19. Hydraulic system
20. Main corridor
21. Quadex power core
22. Gun turret access
23. Quad laser turret
24. Main hold
25. Holographic game board
26. Water recycling unit
27. Subspace radio
28. Sensor array controller/ interpreter
29. Sensor array
30. Concussion missiles
31. Deflector shield generator
32. Anti-concussion field generator
33. Landing jet
34. Passive sensor antenna
35. Tractor beam projector
36. Imperial IFF transponder
37. Forward hold
38. Freight-loading room
39. Number two hold
40. Life support systems
41. Secret compartments
42. Cockpit access corridor
43. Cockpit

A notoriously charming man with a lifelong dedication to all things extravagant, Lando Calrissian is perhaps best known as a hero of the Rebel Alliance. His many careers have included interstellar grifter, smuggler, and professional gambler, especially proficient at the high-stakes card game sabacc. For years he was a regular fixture of the gambling tournaments at Cloud City, the floating metropolis in the atmosphere of the gas planet Bespin. He was also once the owner of the *Millennium Falcon*.

Although Calrissian's bestselling memoir, *How to Succeed in Everything*, does not divulge details of how he obtained the *Falcon*, Cloud City Sabacc Tournament (CCSB) records indicate he won the freighter from its previous owner, Cix Trouvee, during the third day of a competition at the Yarith Bespin Hotel. However, it should be noted that CCSB records are sometimes unreliable, as many were revised for discretionary purposes or 'creative accounting'. By all accounts, Cix Trouvee was a capable pilot but an incorrigible gambler, and had been overwhelmed by the constant maintenance requirements for his YT-1300. Fortunately for Trouvee, his financial circumstances improved dramatically soon after he lost the *Falcon*, and he became the vice president of Planet Dreams, Inc. a very successful entertainment consortium based on Oseon VII.

Because Calrissian was a novice pilot at the time he acquired the *Falcon*, he enlisted a tutor, the Corellian pilot Han Solo, who already had a reputation as one of the best star jockeys in all of Hutt Space. Calrissian was a quick study, but the challenges of maneuvering a freighter on his own were daunting, and he realized he required a co-pilot.

His quest for a co-pilot ended by way of a gambling match, after Calrissian won a bizarre starfish-shaped droid named Vuffi Raa. Equipped with five articulated tentacles, Vuffi Raa became Calrissian's ally on several adventures, deftly helping him evade Imperial starships, pirates, and other threats. Calrissian used profits from one escapade to purchase a used-starship lot on Nar Shaddaa. He parted ways with Vuffi Raa under incredible circumstances at the ThonBoka, a nebula in the Centrality.

Leaving the *Millennium Falcon* on Nar Shaddaa, Calrissian traveled by luxury liner to Cloud City for the

Sabacc Tournament. At the gaming tables, he was reunited with Han Solo, who happened to be a relatively amateur sabacc player, and both made it to the final championship round. During that round Calrissian found himself short of credits, and he placed 'any ship' on his Nar Shaddaa lot as his marker. Incredibly, Solo won the hand, and Calrissian was further chagrined when Solo claimed the *Falcon*. According to various sources, Calrissian never intended to bet the *Falcon*, nor imagined that Solo had any idea that the YT-1300 was in the lot at the time. Although Calrissian did not question Solo's cards, he also did not regard Solo's acquisition of the *Falcon* as entirely fair, which caused a rift in their friendship for years.

Fortunately, Calrissian's time behind the *Falcon*'s controls had been well spent. He was traveling in a different freighter when he took the opportunity to single-handedly defeat the Norulac pirates in a skirmish that became known as the Battle of Taanab. Not surprisingly, Calrissian had an ulterior motive for vanquishing the pirates, as his victory added a Clendoran brewery to his growing list of business operations.

At yet another Cloud City Sabacc Tournament, Calrissian accomplished perhaps his greatest gambling feat when he played against Cloud City's Baron Administrator. When the game was over, Calrissian had won the title of Baron Administrator along with all the power that went with it. Despite having spent so many years living as a rogue, he took his new position very seriously. He improved living conditions for all citizens, increased profits for the Tibanna gas-mining operations, protected the city from pirate raids, and did his best to discourage the Empire from having any proprietary interest in Cloud City.

Eventually, however, Cloud City came to the attention of the Emperor's own lieutenant, the Sith Lord Darth Vader. Vader had taken a special interest in the *Millennium Falcon* because her crew had played no small part in a battle that had destroyed the Empire's superweapon, the Death Star. Having learned that the *Falcon* was en route to Cloud City, Vader arrived in advance with Imperial stormtroopers. After Han Solo and his Wookiee co-pilot, Chewbacca, landed the *Falcon* at Cloud City, Vader turned Solo over to a bounty hunter, and Calrissian was forced to make some hard decisions

about his allegiances. Ultimately, he chose to side with the Rebels.

Knowing that the bounty hunter had delivered Solo to Jabba the Hutt, a crime lord on the sand planet Tatooine, Calrissian and Chewbacca flew the *Falcon* to Tatooine and worked with other Rebels to rescue him. Later, when the Rebels learned the Empire had a second Death Star under construction in the Endor system, Solo led a small Rebel contingent to the forest moon of Endor while Calrissian—piloting the *Falcon*—led the starfighter assault on the unfinished Imperial battle station. Calrissian's co-pilot was Nien Nunb, a Sullustan. During the battle, Calrissian convinced Alliance leader Admiral Ackbar to move closer to the Imperial fleet, a strategy that saved countless Rebels because it effectively discouraged the Imperials from firing their battle station's superlaser within such close range of their own vessels.

While Ackbar held off the Imperial starships, Calrissian and Rebel X-wing pilot Wedge Antilles flew through the narrow passages of the Death Star's superstructure to reach the incomplete station's reactor core. Antilles and Calrissian fired missiles that shattered the core and caused a chain reaction that sent waves of massive explosions through the entire battle station. During a hasty retreat, the *Falcon*'s rectenna dish struck a girder and shattered. Calrissian and his Rebel allies managed to outrun the explosions, and successfully destroyed the Imperial superweapon.

Calrissian returned the *Falcon* to Han Solo, who was relieved to see the Corellian freighter was mostly unscathed. Following the Battle of Endor, Calrissian returned to Cloud City, where he led 'Lando's Commandos' to drive the remaining Imperial forces out of the Bespin system.

↑ The Sullustan Nien Nunb in the co-pilot's seat beside Lando Calrissian in the *Millennium Falcon*'s cockpit during the Battle of Endor. After the battle, Nunb temporarily served as co-pilot with Han Solo while Chewbacca visited family on Kashyyyk.

Boasting a life filled with more notorious experiences than Lando Calrissian could claim, the Corellian pilot Han Solo had such a shady past that it was almost impossible for anyone to imagine he might come to be regarded as a hero, let alone respectable. And where Calrissian left countless people feeling grateful as he emptied their vaults and bank accounts, Solo left a trail of vengeful enemies. Brash, reckless, and easy to anger, he was also a frequent stranger to good manners and had an ego beyond compare. Perhaps the most infuriating aspect of Solo's enormously high opinion of himself was that he actually was one of the best starpilots in the galaxy. His reputation as a pirate, smuggler, and enthusiastic sharpshooter spanned the Outer Rim as well as the Corporate Sector.

According to various sources, Solo had been a career criminal since childhood, when he learned the ways of pickpockets and petty thieves. As a teenager, he raced swoops in competitions before he began flying cargo barges for the Besadii Hutts. Rumor has it he was trying to escape his past when he joined the Imperial Navy. He eventually graduated at the top of his class at the Academy, serving as a naval officer and fighter pilot.

Despite Solo's tough exterior, roguish ways, and disrespect for authority in general, he had another side that he did little to promote: an affinity for lost causes and underdogs. Although details are sketchy, a popular story suggests his sympathetic disposition became the undoing of his military service when he disobeyed orders and rescued a Wookiee captive from brutal Imperials. Solo was summarily kicked out of the Navy, but his discharge came with an unexpected bonus: the liberated Wookiee, allegedly obliged by ancient tradition, became his rescuer's companion and guardian. The Wookiee's name was Chewbacca.

Nearly 200 years old at the time he met Solo, Chewbacca was a native of the planet Kashyyyk. A veteran of the Clone Wars, he fought alongside the Jedi Master Yoda against an invasion of Confederacy droids at the Battle of Kashyyyk, and was an expert shot with a Wookiee bowcaster. Along with his strength and fighting skills, Chewbacca was an able pilot and mechanic, with extensive experience in starship repair.

Solo and Chewbacca made a formidable team, and quickly gained a reputation as smugglers in the criminal underworld of Nar Shaddaa, where they maintained a hideout. Using leased or borrowed ships, they ran spice—a product of the planet Kessel's labor mines—for the Desilijic clan, of which Jabba the Hutt was a member. But from the moment Solo first laid eyes on Lando Calrissian's battered YT-1300 freighter, he knew he was fated to own the *Millennium Falcon*. Solo literally played his cards right, and the *Falcon* became his.

Deciding to put some distance between themselves and the Empire, Solo and Chewbacca flew the *Falcon* to Kashyyyk, where Chewbacca married a beautiful Wookiee named Mallatobuck. The wedding surprised Solo because he knew Chewbacca had no immediate intentions of remaining on Kashyyyk, but he knew better than to question his friend about such things.

Solo and Chewbacca proceeded to the Corporate

↗ **Han Solo and Chewbacca meet Ben Kenobi and Luke Skywalker in the Mos Eisley Cantina on Tatooine.**

→ **After killing a bounty hunter in self-defense, Han Solo faces the greedy gangster Jabba the Hutt in Docking Bay 94.**

⬇ **After infiltrating the Death Star battle station, Han Solo and Chewbacca agree to help Luke Skywalker rescue a captive princess.**

⬂ **Inside the Death Star docking bay that holds the *Falcon*, Solo and Chewbacca fire at stormtroopers as they make a daring escape.**

Sector, a region of the galaxy operated by a private corporation, the Corporate Sector Authority, which was granted a charter by the Empire to exploit all the resources of tens of thousands of star systems. Technically and legally, the Authority was owner, employer, landlord, government, and military, and by no means benevolent. Naturally, Solo and Chewbacca were determined to fleece the Authority. Also naturally, nothing went exactly as planned.

After seeking help from Klaus 'Doc' Vandangante's team of outlaw techs to upgrade the *Falcon*, Solo and Chewbacca wound up rescuing Doc from the Authority prison planet known as Stars' End. They had a nasty run-in with slavers, but managed to bring the fiends to something almost like justice *and* make a profit. Leaving Authority space, they went to the planet Dellalt in the Tion Hegemony, where they helped recover the legendary treasure of Xim the Despot.

But money never lasted long with Solo and Chewbacca, as the *Falcon* demanded constant and often expensive maintenance. They went to Tatooine, docked their ship at Mos Eisley Spaceport, and began working somewhat steadily for Jabba the Hutt. Jabba sent them on numerous odd jobs, but most often had them run spice from Kessel. But when an Imperial patrol intercepted one run, Solo jettisoned an entire load of spice before the Imperials boarded the *Falcon*. Although Solo avoided arrest, Jabba was not pleased about the lost revenue, and expected Solo to pay him. Because Solo was among the best smugglers, Jabba gave him time to raise the necessary credits. But Jabba was not a patient fellow, and he soon notified his henchmen that he had placed a bounty on Solo.

Solo and Chewbacca believed their luck had turned for the better when a lightsaber-wielding old man named Ben Kenobi and his farmboy companion Luke Skywalker entered a Mos Eisley cantina, looking for a pilot to take them and a pair of droids to the planet Alderaan in exchange for 17,000 credits. But the *Falcon*'s crew got more than they bargained for.

Imperial troops and Star Destroyers tried to stop the *Falcon* from leaving Tatooine. Jumping into hyperspace, Solo and Chewbacca escaped with their passengers to Alderaan, only to discover that their destination had been completely destroyed. And then a lone Imperial

TIE fighter lured the *Falcon* to a moon-sized Imperial battle station, the Death Star, which used a powerful tractor beam to snare the Corellian freighter.

After infiltrating the Death Star and evading capture, Solo and Chewbacca learned the Rebel leader Princess Leia Organa was being held prisoner on the battle station. With visions of a huge reward dancing in their heads, the *Falcon*'s crew agreed to help Skywalker liberate the princess. Against all odds, they succeeded, and delivered her to a Rebel base in the Yavin system.

And against seemingly larger odds, Solo revealed that he was not a total mercenary. Although Solo had claimed his only interest in rescuing Princess Leia was for the reward, and that he wanted no part in assisting the Rebels, when the Death Star arrived at Yavin, Solo and Chewbacca did not abandon their new allies.

↗ **Standing in a maintenance bay located below the deck of the *Falcon*'s main hold, Chewbacca makes emergency repairs.**

➡ **Following the Battle of Yavin, the Rebel Alliance honors Han Solo, Chewbacca, and Luke Skywalker for their courage.**

⬇ **Shortly after the Empire crushed the Rebel base on Hoth, Princess Leia begins to yield to Han Solo's charms while aboard the *Falcon*.**

↘ **Lando Calrissian, Chewbacca, Solo, and Leia listen to Rebel leaders outline a plan to attack an Imperial battle station in the Endor system.**

PILOTING A YT-1300

From the
CEC YT-1300 Marketing Catalog

Although the YT-1300 is equipped with numerous automated systems to help a small crew operate the entire ship, Corellian Engineering Corporation does not expect any pilots to rely too much on mechanized support when they get behind the flight controls. Why? Because even though CEC offers conversion kits that can transform almost any ship into a drone barge, the YT-1300 doesn't fly like any other transport in its class. Some say it's not like any other ship at all.

Don't believe us? Consider this report from *Starship and Pilot* journalist Bali Rayden: 'I've tested a lot of CEC ships and more freighters than I can name. I can't say I was expecting any big surprises from the YT-1300. I knew it would have some muscle and assumed it would handle well. But after taking the standard freighter model out for a run and a few spins, I was amazed at the ship's maneuverability, how it handled more like a snubfighter than a light transport. I returned to the CEC flight-test facility with something very unexpected. A grin so big it made my face ache. Of all the ships I've ever flown, I can honestly say the YT-1300 is the most *fun*.'

Measel Junco, famed long-hauler and esteemed columnist for the *Independent Traders' Infonet*, had this to say: 'Ever since I recently announced my intention to retire my route on the Corellian Trade Spine, I've received many kind messages from friends and fellow long-haulers. However, I made that announcement before CEC invited me to climb into the cockpit of the YT-1300. Now, here's a new announcement. I plan to continue flying my route for as long as I'm able, and I won't add "or as long as my brand new YT-1300 holds up" because that would be a disservice to a ship that will undoubtedly survive this old cyborg. If I ever do retire, I might just install a deluxe crew cabin, because I don't ever want to stray too far from that cockpit.'

CEC designers, engineers, technicians, and assembly workers know that when you get behind the controls of the YT-1300, you'll be ready for launch too. CEC encourages all pilots to visit your local CEC ship dealer or authorized CEC reseller, where on-premise flight simulators will familiarize you with the unique challenges of operating this new freighter.

The *Millennium Falcon* leads two X-wing starfighters through the second Death Star's superstructure at the Battle of Endor.

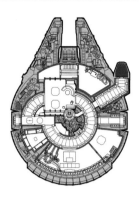

The *Millennium Falcon*'s cockpit features a large transparisteel window, and holds four swivel-mounted seats. In front, the pilot's and co-pilot's seats are positioned before a console of controls and data displays; both seats can be adjusted for comfort. The two rear seats were installed by a previous owner. All seats have safety belts.

To reduce expenses and increase efficiency, Han Solo rigged many of the *Falcon*'s essential systems—navigational, communications, defensive, life-support, and weapons—through the master control panels in the main hold's technical station and the cockpit; if necessary, one person can operate the ship from either location. The rigging and additional modifications have transformed the *Millennium Falcon*'s cockpit control console into a cluster of switches, buttons, and scopes that would intimidate all but the most experienced spacer.

Dual control yokes were a standard feature for the stock YT-1300. The *Falcon*'s yokes have articulated

mounts and have been reinforced to accommodate Chewbacca's considerable strength. The yokes also have push-button controls for press-to-talk comm systems and tactical maneuvering.

The central display monitor can be adjusted to present a selected range of data for navigation, communications, and defense. This data includes star charts, sensor scans of nearby starships, and energy readouts that allow the pilots to determine whether energy needs to be rerouted to engines or shields. Because the central display monitor is typically programmed to display data about enemy vessels and other hazards, it is commonly referred to as the 'threat screen'. Other scopes present dedicated sensor data and status indicators.

The cockpit console is equipped with a socket for an astromech droid's scomp link, which allows a droid to insert jump coordinates and—if necessary—control the ship. Similar scomp links are also built into the *Falcon*'s technical and engineering stations.

⬇ **Inside the *Falcon*'s cockpit, Han Solo and Chewbacca operate the controls while Princess Leia and the protocol droid C-3PO sit behind them.**

1. Distress beacon
2. Orbital maneuvering display system
3. Combat maneuver panel
4. Sensors
5. Comlink
6. Control yoke
7. Engine start levers
8. Turn and bank indicator
9. Weapons
10. Display monitor
11. Throttle
12. Sublight engines
13. Velocity indicator
14. Auxiliary power
15. Hyperdrive
16. Speed brake handle
17. Autopilot switch
18. Warning light
19. Landing gear
20. Deflector shield controls
21. Shield status display
22. Subspace radio
23. Acceleration compensator display
24. Transparisteel window

↑ With the *Falcon* in need of repair, her crew cautiously allows Bespin Wing Guard cloud cars to escort them to Cloud City.

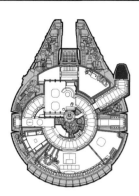

The aft bulkheads of the *Millennium Falcon*'s cockpit are covered with instrument lighting, gauges, and control switches for systems throughout the ship, including navigation and propulsion. The hatch that separates the cockpit from a passage tube (the access corridor that leads to the circular main corridor) can be sealed. Taller pilots and passengers must duck as they move through the hatch. If the instrument lighting fails during start-up procedures, CEC does not recommend striking the aft bulkhead to make the lighting stay on.

➜ On an ill-fated journey to the planet Alderaan, Chewbacca, Luke Skywalker, Ben Kenobi, and Han Solo instead discover the Death Star.

⬇ Han Solo checks the *Falcon*'s nav computer as he prepares for lift-off.

COMMUNICATIONS

The *Millennium Falcon*'s crew relies on a number of communications systems. To maintain contact inside and outside the *Falcon*, both Han Solo and Chewbacca carry small short-range two-way communication devices called comlinks. For hands-free conversations, intercoms are hard-wired into stations throughout the ship.

In addition to a standard subspace radio, which has a limited range of only a few light years, the *Falcon* is equipped with a Chedak Frequency Agile subspace transceiver. A relatively common device, the Chedak allows faster-than-light audio, video, and hologram communications, and is also used to broadcast distress signals and other emergency messages. The transceiver's subspace antenna has 12km of tightly wound, ultrathin superconducting wire that allows it to achieve a broadcast range of approximately 40 light years. The Chedak's receiver automatically monitors standard clear frequencies for distress signals and hailing messages from nearby vessels. Han Solo has added a Carbanti Whistler encryption module, but uses the unit sparingly because subspace messages can be intercepted by any vessel within the transceiver's considerable broadcast range.

ANTI-BOARDING SYSTEMS

The *Millennium Falcon* has a series of cameras, blast doors, weapons, and other security measures placed throughout the ship, to assist the crew in combating unwanted visitors without directly exposing themselves. All the *Millennium Falcon*'s access systems have inboard overrides, which can make life complicated for anyone interested in forced entry. But after Han Solo temporarily lost the *Falcon* to skillful thieves, he installed a sophisticated anti-theft device with a 'delayed response' default mode. This device relies on retina scans of the ship's systems operator, and palmprint identification via the instrument panel steering yoke. If a thief manages to bypass the other security systems and launch the *Falcon*, the first attempt to employ the sublight engine or hyperdrive automatically triggers a default that sends the ship directly back to the place from which it was launched.

1 Nav computer
2 Navigational display
3 Data slot
4 Hyperdrive systems status
5 Subspace engines status
6 Power systems indicators
7 Reinforced bulkhead
8 Hatch
9 Hatch control switch
10 Fuel management panel
11 Environmental controls
12 Cabin pressure altimeter
13 Air supply/flow controls
14 Situation display indicators
15 Integrated control panels

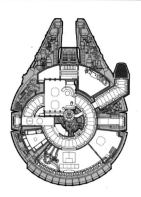

The navigational computer is the key component in any starship's navigational system. Commonly known as a nav computer or navicomputer, this component works in conjunction with the hyperdrive and sensor systems to calculate realspace trajectories as well as light-speed jumps and safe journeys along known hyperspace routes. They hold a tremendous amount of data, storing locations of stars, planets, asteroid fields, debris, gas clouds, gravity wells, and other hazards, all of which are moving through space. Nav computers also have complex mapping functions for determining safe routes over land or atmosphere environments.

The Space Ministry is constantly updating and recalculating well-known hyperspace routes and astrogation charts, and makes the data available to starships' navicomputers. The ministry's updating process includes routinely collecting route and sensor data from navicomputers when ships dock at spaceports, and the ministry offers data on new routes after they are safely tested. According to authorities, only about a quarter of the galaxy has been properly surveyed, and some experts estimate that the locations of more than 90% of all large bodies in the galaxy remain unknown.

The *Millennium Falcon* still relies upon its factory-issued Microaxial Rubicon astrogation computer. Considered state-of-the-art when the YT-1300 was brand new, the Rubicon still crunches data faster than most late-model astromech droids. Like most CEC components, it is sturdy and easy to upgrade. Han Solo and Chewbacca have added memory nodules to accommodate data for virtually unlimited jump calculations for numerous star systems.

Like most smart starhoppers, the *Falcon*'s crew keeps an up-to-date clone of the Rubicon separate from the ship systems. The clone is a rebuilt Microaxial HyD modular nav computer, which is housed in a compartment near the aft engineering station. In the event of the backup nav computer failing, the *Falcon* also has a strongbox bolted to the underside of the main hold's engineering-station console; this strongbox contains a simple astrogation plotter and star charts that include the galaxy's pulsars and variable stars, each of which has a unique signature. With these tools, spacers can calculate their own location as well as a path to the nearest habitable world or spaceport.

↑ On the run from the Imperial fleet, Han Solo plots a course for the Bespin system.

→ Far from Imperial space, Lando Calrissian and Chewbacca steer the *Falcon* away from the Rebel fleet.

1 Holographic astrogation display
2 Target destination
3 Security scanner
4 Event timer
5 Mission timer
6 Course selection/confirmation keys
7 Manual override
8 Course plotter display
9 Attitude indicators
10 Main housing
11 Holoprojector
12 Holographic systems casing

Hyperspace travel has been part of everyday life for so many millennia, it's hard to imagine our galactic community without the ability to journey from one star system to another in just a few hours or days. In fact, a series of historic surveys show spacefarers have been taking hyperspace travel for granted for generations, and many are oblivious of the technology that makes such travel possible. Despite this almost universally relaxed attitude, any astrophysicist or hyperspace technician will tell you that the dangers of hyperspace travel should never be underestimated.

For those who are unfamiliar with hyperspace, it is a dimension of space-time that can be entered only at faster-than-light speeds. While the most knowledgeable astrophysicists and astrogation experts admit that some aspects of hyperspace remain a mystery, it is understood that hyperspace is coterminous with realspace: each point in realspace is associated with a unique point in hyperspace, and adjacent points in realspace are adjacent in hyperspace. In other words, if you travel 'north' in realspace as you jump into hyperspace, you will head 'north' into hyperspace too.

Also, every object in realspace has a 'shadow' in hyperspace. For example, there is a star (or star-like body) in hyperspace at the same location as it occupies in realspace. Such 'shadows' are potentially lethal obstacles for travelers in hyperspace, which is why pilots rely on astrogation computers to plot courses around the mass shadows, allowing travel from one point in realspace to another. Consider the fact that the known galaxy has approximately 400 billion stars and 180 billion star systems, billions of planets,

➜ Racing away from an Imperial armada, Han Solo makes final checks on the *Falcon*'s flight systems before launching into hyperspace.

➜ Almost immediately after the *Falcon*'s hyperdrive kicks in, stars visible outside the *Falcon*'s cockpit canopy appear to elongate and radiate from a central 'target' point of trajectory.

innumerable asteroids, and that none of these bodies are stationary. Without the careful calculations of astrogation computers, a starship could very easily wind up smashing into a star or planet. Only a desperate or foolhardy pilot would attempt a hyperspace jump to any location without up-to-date astrogation charts and astrogation droids or computers.

So why risk traveling through hyperspace? The simple answer is time itself. Without hyperspace technology, interstellar travel requires more time than most species care to sacrifice. The earliest space travelers utilized cybernetic hibernation and 'sleeper ships' for even 'short' intrasystem flights so that they could preserve the duration of their own natural lives while avoiding years or decades of monotonous activity within their vessels' confines.

For those who remain concerned about the hazards of space travel, safety experts are quick to note that millions of hyperspace jumps are made *daily*, and only a small fraction of jumps fail. Furthermore, nearly all failures are due to operator error. The experts agree that the best way to ensure a safe journey through hyperspace is to use only the highest-quality technology, keep it properly maintained, and obey all safety protocols.

Corellian Engineering Corporation has been at the forefront of space-travel technology for thousands of years, and has consistently received more quality-control awards from *Starship and Pilot* than any other manufacturer. No matter where you travel through hyperspace, a CEC ship will get you where you want to go.

3

← While starlight becomes even more distorted, the *Falcon*'s energy shields, sensors, and other technology work in tandem to make the crew and passengers feel relatively unaffected by the ship's incredible speed.

4

← In a matter of seconds, the *Falcon* moves into faster-than-light-speed and jumps into hyperspace.

When the YT-1300 was first released, CEC's promotional campaign encouraged pilots to visit any major CEC dealer or authorized reseller with on-premise flight simulators before purchasing a YT-1300. The simulators, CEC maintained, would allow pilots an opportunity to familiarize themselves with 'the unique challenges' of operating the new freighter.

This 'encouragement' was actually part of a cagey CEC marketing strategy, designed not only to generate interest in the YT-1300, but to promote the idea that the YT-1300 was more than the average pilot could handle. The strategy worked, as thousands of pilots not only tested the flight simulators but left the CEC dealer with a new YT-1300. While inexperienced pilots are typically curious about the degree of difficulty involved in operating a wide freighter with a starboard-mounted cockpit, most experienced pilots maintain that the so-called challenges are no different than flying any ship with sections that extend beyond the pilot's visual range.

According to CEC's guidelines for flying the YT-1300, engines should warm up for approximately three minutes before initiating the repulsorlift drive for lift-off.

CEC recommends the same amount of time for starting the sublight drive and up to several minutes or more for the hyperdrive, depending on the complexity of the calculations required by the navicomputer. Although starting any other YT-1300 before such preliminary warm-ups could wreak havoc on a ship's systems, Han Solo's modifications enable the *Millennium Falcon* to launch from a planet or space station within 20 seconds of starting the engines, and can usually launch the *Falcon* into hyperspace with less than three minutes of prep time.

The cockpit's dual control yokes are similar to the controls on most starships: to ascend, pull back on the yoke; to descend, push the yoke forward. Rotating the yoke controls both pitch and roll, and a small side-stick is used for tight turns and rolls. The throttle sets the desired power level: push the throttle to increase speed, and pull back to decelerate. The deceleration controls are linked to the *Falcon*'s attitude and braking thrusters, which work in conjunction with the ship's thrust-regulating alluvial dampers. In the hands of an especially skilled pilot, these simple controls can transform the bulky YT-1300 into a nimble and elusive flyer.

⬇ **Chewbacca and Princess Leia steer the *Falcon* away from Imperial TIE fighters as they leave the Bespin system.**

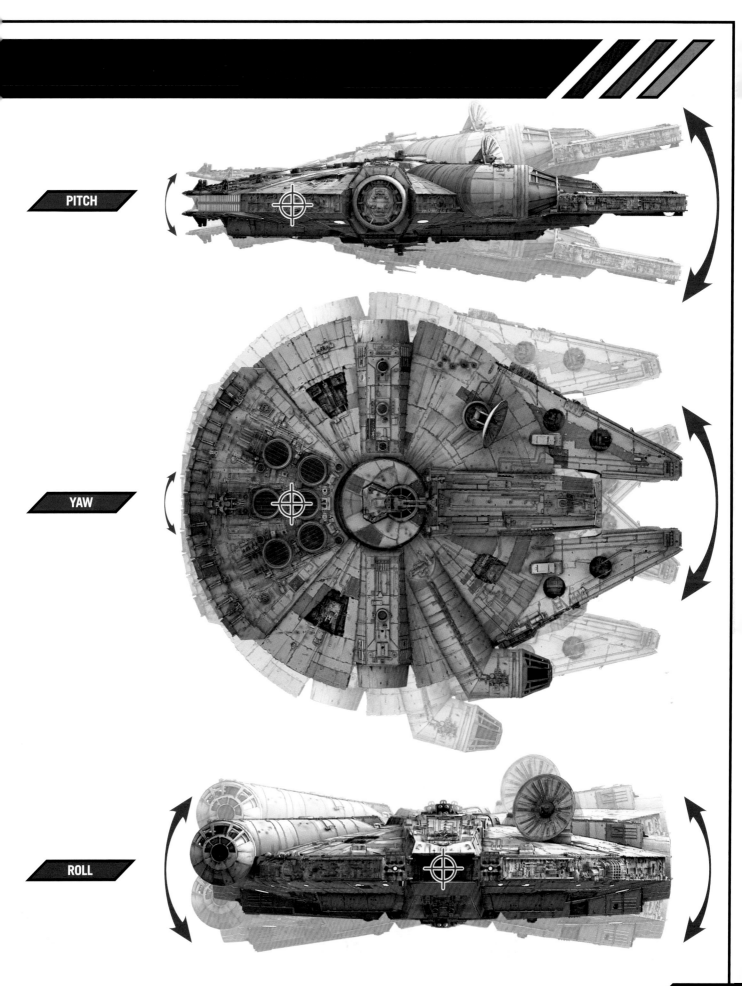

PITCH

YAW

ROLL

During his education at the Imperial Academy, Han Solo studied the Imperial-issued *Treatise on Starfighter Tactics* by the legendary tactician Adar Tallon. According to Tallon, starfighter combat can be broken up into five stages: *detection, closing, attack, maneuver,* and *disengagement.* Despite the fact that the *Treatise* was meant primarily for pilots of small starfighters, and specifically TIE fighters, Solo found some of Tallon's observations and instructions useful when the *Millennium Falcon* encountered enemy ships. And because most Imperial pilots were unaware of Solo's military experience, they were typically unprepared when he used their own tactics against them.

In *detection,* the first stage of starfighter combat, possible threats are detected either visually or by electronic means. After a target is detected, it must be positively identified. The *Falcon*'s sensors and long-range scanners easily detect other vessels, which are almost immediately identified by the *Falcon*'s data-sorting computer. However, because some enemies use sensor-jamming technology or are skilled at concealment, both Solo and Chewbacca know better than to rely too heavily on technology for detecting other ships. They believe it's imperative to keep their eyes open while in the cockpit, and do their best to make sure at least one of them is always in the cockpit when traveling at sublight speed. As Tallon noted in his *Treatise*: 'Eyes cannot easily be jammed, altered, or otherwise interfered with.'

Although Han Solo has a reputation as an occasionally trigger-happy smuggler, he generally prefers to avoid space battles by outrunning or tricking his opponents. If evasion is not an option, he may proceed to engage the enemy, which is consistent with Tallon's second stage: the attempt to attain an advantageous position for an attack run is known as

⬇ **After the Battle of Hoth, Han Solo flies the** *Millennium Falcon* **to the surface of a large asteroid to evade Imperial TIE fighters.**

closing. The two essential elements of closing are speed and concealment, as both aid in limiting the amount of time the opponent has to react to the attack. With the *Falcon*, speed is usually only an issue if the hyperdrive malfunctions. Concealment can be difficult to achieve against sophisticated Imperial sensors, but the *Falcon*'s powerful sensor-jammers *can* jam transmissions from small Imperial fighters. If concealment fails, one can attempt to deceive an opponent by using one of the *Falcon*'s false transponder codes to pretend to be a different ship, all the while moving in fast at the target.

The single most decisive stage of starfighter combat is the *attack* stage, which accounts for four out of every five starfighter kills. A head-on attack will almost always result in a quick victory for one pilot or the other. According to Tallon's *Treatise*, 'the one who gets in the first telling shot wins'. However, the *Falcon* has powerful deflector shields, and TIE fighters do not, which gives

the *Falcon* an additional advantage. Still, the best avenue for attack is usually to approach the enemy from astern. The closer an attacker angles into the intended target's stern, the better shot he will get. Tallon refers to this vulnerable target area as the 'prime target cone'.

The *maneuver* stage of combat occurs only when a pilot's initial onset fails, and the pilot finds himself under attack. This can result in a dogfight. In maneuvering out of an attack, the first priority is to survive, and the second is to turn the tables on the enemy, ideally by attacking the target's stern. The first pilot who makes a mistake is almost always the loser.

Tallon does not mince words regarding the final stage of combat, *disengagement*: 'The inexperienced pilot frequently believes that following an attack pass, particularly a successful one, the engagement is over and he can relax. This is dangerous nonsense.' Tallon notes that the longer a pilot remains in the combat area, the more vulnerable he is to being swarmed by incoming fighters. If possible, a plan for disengagement should be considered before an attack is commenced. Unless the enemy is completely destroyed, the most effective method of disengagement is to angle off at full-throttle and escape into hyperspace.

Han Solo knows a few tricks that Adar Tallon never imagined, but he has yet to write a book about them.

↑ At the Battle of Endor, Lando Calrissian brings the *Falcon* into the midst of the Imperial fleet, prompting the larger warships to hold their fire or risk destroying their own vessels.

GRAVITY ASSISTS

When traveling at sublight speed through planetary systems, a practical way to conserve energy, fuel expenses, and time is to use a gravity assist. Also called a gravitational slingshot or swing-by, a gravity assist takes advantage of the natural gravitational forces of planets, moons, and other large celestial bodies to allow starships to change speed or trajectory.

As a ship approaches a planet, the planet's gravity pulls at the ship and alters its speed. The ship's angle of approach—passing either behind or in front of the planet, relative to the planet's orientation to its sun—will determine how much the ship will accelerate or decelerate. Navigational computers calculate the ship's speed and trajectory in combination with the planet's gravity and the gravitational force from the nearest sun, and can determine the most economical route—typically a precise elliptical path—to enter the planet's orbit or redirect the ship away from the planet's gravitational influence.

The most commonly used gravity assists are for decelerating upon arrival into planetary orbit, and also decelerating through a planet's atmosphere. Gravity assists are also used to divert and deliver ships to hyperspace portals, but extra calculations must be made to ensure that the ships enter the portals at the correct trajectory.

Stars can also be used for gravity assists to greatly magnify a ship's thrusting power. Most pilots eschew this method because flying so close to a star requires nearly all of a ship's energy to be diverted to its deflector shields. In fact, a 'solar slingshot' is usually only dared by desperate pirates and spacers who can endure extremely high levels of radiation exposure.

To decelerate, a spacecraft passes over a planet's pole to move 'behind' the planet.

To accelerate, a spacecraft wraps around the equator to pass 'in front' of the planet.

EVADING A TRACTOR BEAM

If an enemy ship's tractor beam locks on to your own vessel, you have three options: surrender, attack, or take drastic action to quickly convince the enemy to release you. If surrender is not an option, the decision to attack is generally based on which ship has superior firepower, how fast you can target and destroy the enemy's tractor beam projectors, and whether your ship's shields can sustain a close-proximity battle. Remember, an enemy tractor beam doesn't deactivate your own weapons systems, but firing a torpedo is hardly practical if your own ship is too close to the target.

As for drastic action, deliberately accelerating straight for the enemy's ship is a potentially suicidal maneuver. If you suspect your enemy has slow reflexes and little interest in remaining alive, it is probable that your own ship will sustain heavy damage in a collision and possibly be destroyed entirely, taking you with it. But if your enemy consists of an experienced crew who hope to live another day, they will likely shut down the tractor beam, allowing you the chance to break away from their ship.

A marginally safer but also more challenging alternative to the head-on approach is to turn about so that you're facing the enemy ship, increase power to thrusters and shields, then accelerate in a close-pass trajectory past the enemy's tractor beam projector. This action uses both the tractor's draw and your own ship's thrust to effectively reverse the field in the tractor beam, allowing you to snap-roll free of the beam. Although this maneuver is difficult to execute and can severely strain and damage shield generators, it has been known to work.

The *Falcon* accelerates straight at the Destroyer and makes a close pass at the tractor beam projector to reverse the beam's field.

Snared by the Star Destroyer's tractor beam, the *Millennium Falcon* rotates to face the Destroyer.

The *Falcon* snap-rolls free from the Destroyer.

➔ Pursued by an Imperial armada while flying the *Millennium Falcon* with a non-functional hyperdrive, Han Solo chooses to fly straight toward an Imperial Star Destroyer.

➔ As three Star Destroyers converge on the *Falcon*, Solo—confident that his own ship is far more nimble—veers away fast from the Imperial ships.

➔ Solo's maneuver leaves the Star Destroyers on intersecting trajectories. As the respective Imperial crews struggle to avoid collisions, the *Falcon* flees across space.

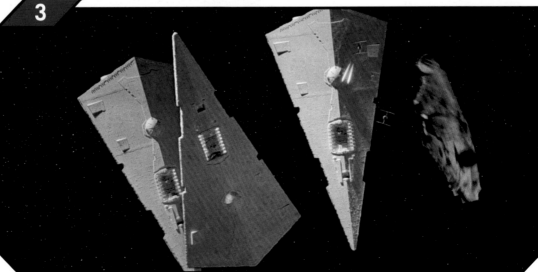

EVADING MULTIPLE SHIPS

During the Battle of Endor, Lando Calrissian, while piloting the *Millennium Falcon*, encouraged the Mon Calamari Admiral Ackbar to move Rebel ships into the midst of the Imperial fleet, a tactic that suddenly forced the enemy to decide whether to hold their fire or risk shooting their own ships. Despite Calrissian having proposed this maneuver, it became known as the *Ackbar slash*. Although Han Solo was on Endor's forest moon during that battle, he is an old hand at a similar tactic to evade multiple ships. Following the Battle of Hoth, Solo outmaneuvered three Imperial Star Destroyers by sending the *Falcon* close between them. In this way he not only temporarily evaded the destroyers, but caused two of them to collide.

Sometimes, the best place to hide a starship is on a much larger starship. In an especially daring maneuver, Han Solo 'concealed' the *Millennium Falcon* from an Imperial armada by racing toward one Imperial Star Destroyer while switching off the *Falcon*'s active sensors, then killing the engines before he used maneuvering jets to gently but rapidly place his ship against the destroyer's aft section. As the *Falcon*'s landing claw locked on to the destroyer, the YT-1300 had already vanished from Imperial sensors. While some might suggest that it would take a great deal of good fortune to pull off this maneuver, Solo maintains it has nothing to do with luck.

⬇ The *Falcon*'s color and relatively flat profile allow her to blend in against the Star Destroyer's hull, leaving Imperials baffled about her whereabouts.

◤ After Chewbacca releases the *Falcon*'s landing claw, Solo and Princess Leia watch from the cockpit as they fall away from the Star Destroyer.

YT-1300 PROPULSION

From the
CEC YT-1300 Engine Guide, Imperial Edition

Corellian Engineering Corporation is in the business of getting you where you want to go. And because CEC wants to get you there fast *and* safely, all CEC ships are thoroughly tested before they leave the CEC orbital assembly facilities, and are guaranteed to carry the most durable and reliable commercial propulsion systems allowed in Galactic Imperial space.

The YT-1300 was originally equipped with Girodyne SRB42 sublight engines, and also specialized vectrals to redirect thrust. Shortly after the first YT-1300s left the factory, several cases of sublight engine power transfer conduit blowouts and drive system stalls became widely reported, but a thorough investigation attributed each mishap to owner/operator error. While the sublight engines are modifiable for greater speed and energy efficiency, owners are advised to make sure that all modifications are made by CEC-authorized engineers and technicians who work in compliance with Imperial laws. With proper care and routine maintenance, the sublight engines will last for decades, a fact evidenced by the many YT-1300s that retain their original Girodyne engines and systems.

Because the YT-1300 was manufactured decades before the foundation of the Galactic Empire, the ship's original Class 2.0 Corellian Avatar-10 hyperdrive remains legal. A bold venture in engineering, the Avatar-10 was promoted as a universal hyperdrive system compatible with any type of spacecraft. Although critics were quick to point out that the Avatar-10's weight of 15 metric tons prohibited installation into spacecraft that were, by design, too small to accommodate such weight even with industrial repulsorlifts, the Avatar-10 became a popular choice for upgrading older freighters and transports. The 'stock' YT-1300 also came with a Class 12 hyperdrive backup.

Like the sublight engines, the factory-issued YT-1300 hyperdrives are considered very durable, and can be modified and upgraded for energy efficiency. However, all owners must be forewarned that any attempt to modify a hyperdrive to achieve speeds faster than a Class 2.0 is in strict violation of Imperial laws.

← Using the combined power of repulsorlifts and sublight engines, the *Millennium Falcon* rises rapidly away to escape a squad of Imperial stormtroopers at Mos Eisley Spaceport on Tatooine.

HYPERDRIVE

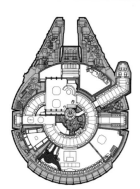

Powered by incredibly efficient fusion generators, hyperdrive engines use a trans-physical effect to launch starships into hyperspace, which can only be entered at faster-than-light speeds. The hyperdrive utilizes supralight 'hypermatter' particles to make the hyperspace jump without changing the ship's complex configuration of mass and energy. To prevent collisions with objects in realspace, an automatic fail-safe will shut down the hyperdrive if sensors detect a gravity field in a ship's navigational path. The hyperdrive can only be engaged when the ship is clear of a stellar body's gravity.

Hyperdrives are categorized by 'class', with lower classes denoting faster speeds. Class 3.0 hyperdrives are common among civilian craft; Class 2.0 or Class 1.0 hyperdrives are typical for most military vessels. Class 0.75 or 0.5 are rare, and usually the result of extensive modifications to existing engines.

The *Millennium Falcon*'s original hyperdrive was a Class 2.0 Corellian Avatar-10. Before Lando Calrissian acquired the *Falcon*, a previous owner had replaced the Avatar-10 with an Isu-Sim SSP05 hyperdrive, which was augmented with numerous parts stolen from a Sienar Fleet Systems prototype Imperial Interdictor cruiser. The stolen parts included a hyperdrive motivator, Rendili transpacitors, paralight relays, and a null quantum field stabilizer. The illegal upgrade more than doubled the hyperdrive's size, and transformed the Isu-Sim into the equivalent of a Class 1.0 hyperdrive.

Like most freighters, the *Falcon* is equipped with an emergency backup hyperdrive, which can be used to limp to the nearest spaceport if the main hyperdrive is disabled. At some point, the YT-1300's original Class 12 backup hyperdrive was upgraded to a Class 10. However, the installation of the military-grade hyperdrive motivator necessitated that both the Isu-Sim SSP05 and backup hyperdrive would share the same single motivator, a modification that can be problematic. If the

❶ **Hyperspace shunt**
❷ **Heat-dissipating vents**
❸ **Effect channels**
❹ **Charge planes**
❺ **Alluvial dampers**
❻ **Field stabilizers**
❼ **High-grade durasteel frame**
❽ **Secondary core processors**
❾ **Titanium-chromium alloy core chamber**
❿ **Power regulators**
⓫ **Inter-level conduits**
⓬ **Horizontal boosters**

motivator is damaged, neither the hyperdrive nor backup hyperdrive will work, and the motivator must be repaired before the *Falcon* can make a hyperspace jump.

After Han Solo acquired the *Falcon*, he brought her to Klaus 'Doc' Vandangante's outlaw techs in the Corporate Sector. Doc's daughter Jessa and her team helped Solo upgrade the hyperdrive to Class 0.5, making the *Falcon* twice as fast as Imperial warships, and also one of the fastest ships in the galaxy. Jury-rigged components and the ship's Quadex power core ensure a three-standard-minute start-up sequence for the hyperdrive.

The *Falcon*'s hyperdrive requires a minimum of eight hours of maintenance per month. Although the Isu-Sim SSP05 hyperdrive generator has been extensively overhauled for energy efficiency, it must be noted that a Class 0.5 hyperdrive is as illegal as it is uncommon. The delicate technology must be very carefully tuned, and tends to malfunction much more often than a standard hyperdrive. There are no such things as standard replacement parts for a Class 0.5 hyperdrive because no manufacturer creates such an unreliable piece of equipment.

The *Falcon*'s hyperdrive has numerous subsystems. A paralight system, a combination of mechanical and opto-electronic subsystems, is responsible for translating a pilot's manual commands into a set of corresponding reactions within the hyperdrive power plants. The hyperdrive engine system has a built-in hyperdrive motivator, the primary lightspeed thrust initiator, which is connected to the main computer system to monitor and collect sensor and navigation data in order to determine jump thrusts, adjust engine performance in hyperspace, and calibrate safe returns to normal space. Horizontal boosters provide energy to the ionization chamber to cause ignition. Alluvial dampers block the emission of ion particles by moving a servo-controlled plate, thus regulating the amount of thrust.

If there's any secret to the performance of the *Falcon*'s hyperdrive, it's Solo's additional—and highly eccentric—modifications to 'streamline' the ship in hyperspace, controlling the warp of the space-time continuum around it. Other ships have attempted to match the *Falcon*'s speed without such modifications, and have exploded into subatomic particles.

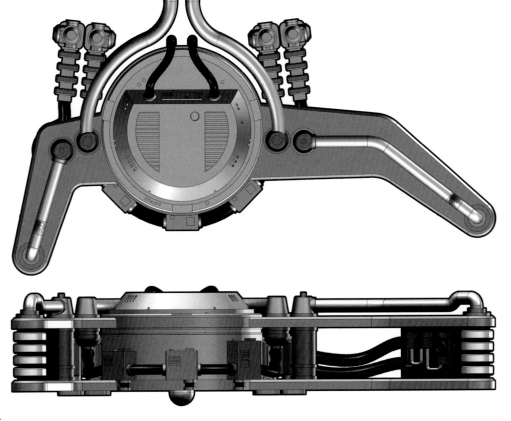

SUBLIGHT DRIVES

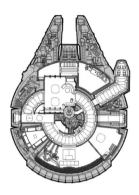

⬇ **Although it is illegal to use sublight drives in atmospheres on populated worlds throughout the galaxy, the law is the least concern of the *Millennium Falcon*'s crew as they escape an Imperial stormtrooper squad on Tatooine.**

Sublight drives, also known as sublight engines, move spacecraft across realspace. They provide more energy output than repulsorlift engines, and are almost always engaged upon leaving a planet's atmosphere and also during space battles. Many varieties of sublight drives exist throughout the galaxy, including solid chemical booster rockets, atomic drives, light sails, and ramjets. Acceleration compensators project appropriately modified gravity effects within a ship to protect pilots and passengers from forceful sublight acceleration. Corellian Engineering Corporation Orbital Facilities have sublight engine test-fire stations to guarantee every CEC ship's sublight engines are fully operational before the ship reaches the consumer.

CEC released the YT-1300 freighter with a pair of Girodyne SRB42 sublight engines. Like most sublight engines, the Girodynes propel the YT-1300 via a fusion reaction that breaks down fuel into charged particles. The resulting energy hurls from the vessel, providing thrust. Thrust vectors redirect this exhaust, and change the ship's trajectory. Because the exhaust is quite hot and mildly radioactive, it is illegal to use such sublight drives in or near the atmospheres of most inhabited facilities and worlds. The radiation requires all CEC technicians who work on vital ion engine components or in the test-fire stations to wear protective gear.

The *Millennium Falcon*'s original Girodyne SRB42 sublight engines have been heavily modified for increased speed. Among the modifications is a sublight acceleration motor (SLAM), an overdrive system designed to draw power from systems not in use to give the ship a brief burst of additional speed.

1. Fuel drive pressure stabilizer
2. Thrust vector plate
3. Actuator
4. Reinforced hull framework
5. Engine room ceiling beam
6. Gas exhaust pre-stabilizer screen
7. Sublight drive exhaust
8. Ignitors
9. Primary thrust pressure manifold
10. Fuel lines
11. Fuel intermixer
12. Reactant injector
13. Power cables
14. Insulator

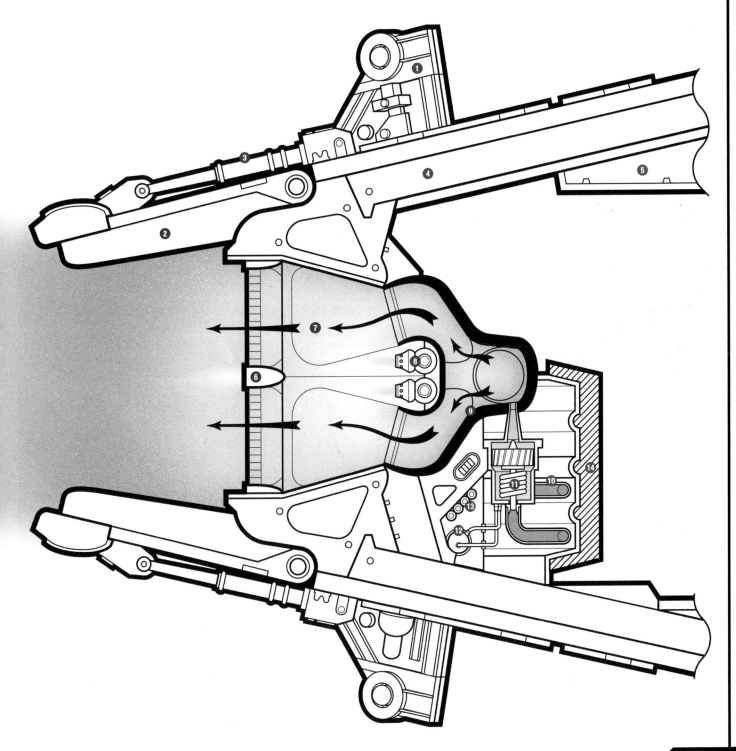

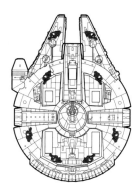

REPULSORLIFT ENGINES

Routinely associated with low-altitude atmospheric vehicles such as landspeeders and speeder bikes, repulsorlift engines, also known as 'antigravs', are used as secondary engines for spacecraft during atmospheric flight and docking procedures. Repulsorlift drive systems utilize a fusion generator, and levitate vehicles via antigravitational emanations called 'repulsor fields', which propel by forming a field of negative gravity that pushes against the natural gravitational field of a planet. The YT-1300 utilizes repulsorlifts in combination with landing jets for planetary lift-offs as well as landings.

Han Solo has augmented the *Falcon's* repulsorlifts with scavenged flux converters and landspeeder turbothrusters. The result of his innovative handiwork is a ship with a higher lift/mass ratio than any CEC engineers would believe possible.

LANDING JETS

The YT-1300's repulsorlift engines have exhaust ducts that divert jet blasts downward through 'landing jet' nozzles located along the lower hull. As their name indicates, the landing jets provide auxiliary thrust and aerostatic lift for landing as well as vertical lift-offs.

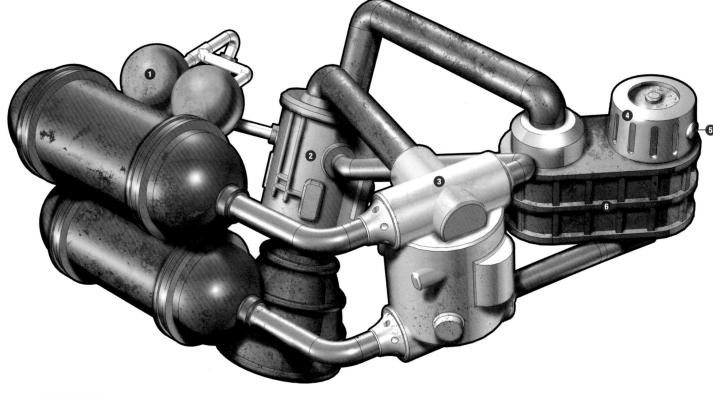

Each landing jet is a swivel-mounted module that automatically adjusts its angle to direct controlled bursts of air or pressurized gas at surfaces below and around the YT-1300 while the landing gear deploys or retracts. Temperature sensors determine how much heat can be released through the jet nozzles without causing any damage to the landing area. Han Solo has modified the landing jets' automatic safety mechanisms so that they *can* release bursts of intense heat, much to the regret of any foe who happens to be too close to the *Falcon*'s lower hull.

1. **Reactant tanks**
2. **Induction housing**
3. **Pressure distributor**
4. **Air intake**
5. **Temperature sensor**
6. **Ionization filter**
7. **Backflow preventer**
8. **Fuel tanks**
9. **Vector control system**
10. **Exhaust nozzle**

LANDING GEAR

Not long before the evacuation of Echo Base on the ice planet Hoth, Solo and Chewbacca extensively renovated the *Falcon*'s undercarriage and landing gear. They added new legs and associated housing structures, and reinforced the hull to withstand additional stresses.

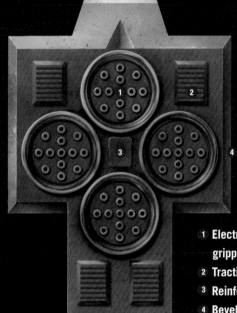

1. **Electromagnetic grippers**
2. **Traction grooves**
3. **Reinforced plating**
4. **Beveled edge**

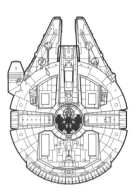

The YT-1300 uses a form of explosive liquid metal fuel that is as energy-efficient as it is hazardous. Developed for the YT-1300 concept ship, the fuel's hazard factor was so controversial that it was almost a reason for CEC to scuttle the entire line. To reduce the risk of explosion, fuel droids are generally used for refueling procedures.

According to the CEC data-keeping department, YT 492727ZED—the serial number for the freighter that evolved into the *Millennium Falcon*—was nearly involved in a calamity before it even left the orbital facility. According to one report, a computer error may have caused a fuel droid to pump an excessive amount of fuel into the freighter while it was still on the assembly line, just before the facility's automated systems guided the freighter into a zero-gravity test area for braking thrusters and attitude jets. Upon entering the test area, the over-fueled freighter, with

its autopilot activated, fired hot and rocketed out of the assembly line, knocking some YT-1300 models aside while sending others spinning, which inadvertently sent two fuel droids into a collision that resulted in an explosion of liquid metal fuel. According to another report, YT 492727ZED reacted 'evasively' to the new and unexpected obstacles in the test area. Fortunately, no lives were lost and damage was minimal, but six Cybot Galactica droid grapplers were ruined before a team of live wranglers gained control of the renegade freighter.

In the *Falcon*'s power core, four fuel slug tanks—each containing radioactive metal used to power the propulsion systems—give her an increased range, even at extreme speeds and engine temperatures. While repairs to the *Falcon*'s various systems must usually be performed each time she lands, she refuels at an average rate of only once per month.

⬇ The frigid temperatures on the planet Hoth required Rebel engineers to modify fuel systems and batteries for spacecraft and other technology, including droids.

1 Line out to power core
2 Return from power core
3 Line out to auxiliary systems
4 Line in from refueling port
5 Fuel distributor
6 Distributor power inlet
7 Fuel tank
8 Tank interchange line
9 Fuel balance regulator
10 Fuel cycler/filter
11 Main line out to engines
12 Fuel delivery pump
13 Pump primer
14 Coolant pump
15 Coolant pump regulator

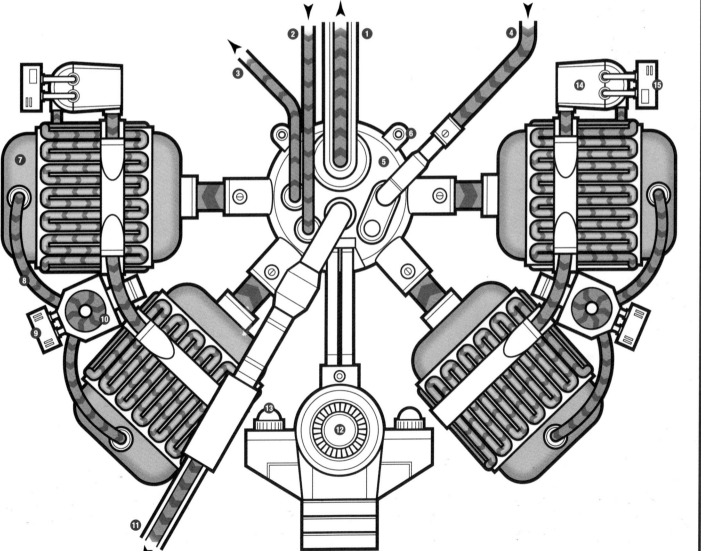

WEAPONS & DEFENSIVE SYSTEMS

From the
*Triplanetary Press History of Space Warfare,
Imperial Edition*

According to ancient records, the galaxy's earliest starship designers were initially concerned about the many natural phenomena that posed dangers to space travelers. Few questioned the fact that energy shields were necessary to protect ships and passengers from radiation and micrometeoroids, or that only ship-mounted laser weapons would give travelers a better chance of survival against rogue asteroids and destructive space-borne creatures. And when one considered the threat of larger asteroids and ferocious monsters that were resistant to laser weapons, one could conclude that ships would be even better defended if they were equipped with missiles.

Inevitably, the proliferation of weapons ensured that the dawn of space travel would bring about the dawn of space warfare. Nuclear, laser, and particle beam weapons spread throughout the galaxy like an insidious disease, and many neighboring worlds and star systems vied for military supremacy. But long after any of those worlds resolved their differences and re-established peace, the routes of space still abounded with pirates, smugglers, and hostile aliens.

Laser cannons became the most common starship weapons in the galaxy. Similar to blasters but much more powerful, laser cannons are powered by either a generator or a direct feed from a ship's main reactor, and use volatile, high-energy blaster gas, which must be stored in supercooled, puncture-proof chambers. A cannon's laser actuator combines the blaster gas with a large power charge, and the actuator's prismatic crystal produces the high-energy beam of charged particles coupled with light. The energy is directed through a long barrel, and the barrel's inner circuitry focuses the beam while increasing its power, allowing the destructive beam to maintain cohesion over great distances.

While high-output laser cannons are legally restricted to military vessels, low-power units are found on most independent freighters and licensed commercial vessels.

The *Millennium Falcon* takes evasive action to escape an armada of Imperial Star Destroyers.

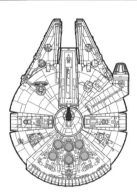

When Lando Calrissian acquired the *Millennium Falcon*, the freighter had a standard Corellian Engineering Corporation twin-gun laser cannon mounted in the dorsal turret. Calrissian replaced the standard twin-gun with a more powerful CEC AG-2G quad laser cannon.

The AG-2G is well known for rapid transverse movement and for a good tight beam for long-range shooting. The gunner uses the horizontal control pedals to rotate the gun left or right, while using the vertical control sticks to point it up or down. The entire turret automatically rotates on a ball-swivel rotation mounting, under the command of the tactical targeting computer. The laser barrels fire one at a time, following a pattern of rotation selected by the gunner. Each barrel fires every 1.32 seconds.

The *Falcon*'s next owner, Han Solo, installed a second turret-mounted AG-2G cannon in the ship's belly. Solo routinely checks the freighter's underside to see that the interrupter-templates have automatically slid into place along the servo-guides for the belly turret. This check ensures the quad-mounted guns won't accidentally blow away the landing gear or boarding ramp if Solo has to fire them while the ship is grounded.

Solo upgraded both cannons by adding enhanced power cyclers, high-volume gas-feeds, and custom-modified laser actuators—with larger energization crystals—for each cannon's barrel, effectively transforming the cannons into military-grade blasters. This highly illegal modification magnifies the laser beam intensity so much that a pursuing light ship, such as an Imperial TIE fighter, can be destroyed with a single hit.

❶ **Access tube**
❷ **Ladder**
❸ **Gunner's seat**
❹ **Twin firing grips with built-in triggers**
❺ **Tactical targeting computer**
❻ **Systems status indicators**
❼ **Maintenance access panels**
❽ **Transparisteel viewport**
❾ **Directional control pedals**
❿ **Rotating platform base**
⓫ **Horizontal support arm**
⓬ **Laser barrels**
⓭ **Tracking servos**
⓮ **Laser cooling unit**
⓯ **Swivel mount**

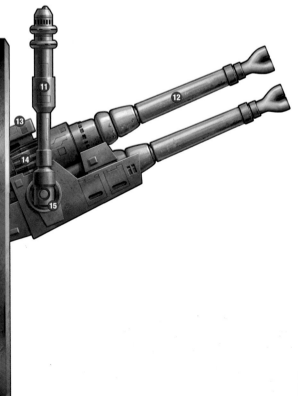

The AG-2G cannons draw energy directly from the *Falcon*'s Quadex power core. The cannons have enhanced cooling packs and compressors for prolonged use without the risk of overheating. The unusual splitter coupling slightly disperses the fired energy beam, forcing the target's shields to deflect energy simultaneously from two hits, which increases the likelihood of overloading the target's shields and inflicting greater damage.

Because of the *Falcon*'s overall design and the position of her main batteries at the precise top and bottom of the ship, her turrets' fields of fire overlap in a wedge that expands from the freighter's mid-section all the way around. Solo and Chewbacca refer to this overlap as the 'Money Lane', as they have a standing wager on who is the better shot with the quad-cannons, and kills scored in the Money Lane carry a double payoff.

QUAD LASER TARGETING COMPUTER

During the fraction of a second that it takes for a skilled gunner to center his sights on a target and pull the trigger, and also the brief time it takes for weapons to energize and fire, a modern starfighter can easily move out of a gunner's sights. Targeting computers compensate for the delay, charting the speed and course of the target and firing just slightly ahead of the point at which the pilot aims.

The *Falcon*'s AG-2G advanced tactical targeting computer is designed to augment the gunner's skill. The advanced computer is accurate up to the longest range of the weapon, and will lock on to any target of greater than 4m in length which stays within scanning range for more than 1.5 seconds. Unfortunately, most Imperial TIE models are fast enough to avoid the 'one-point-five lock', as it is called, leaving AG-2G gunners to rely on their own sharp eyes and steady hands.

REMOTE CONTROLS

Because Calrissian could not be in the *Falcon*'s cockpit and the dorsal turret at the same time, and because his droid co-pilot Vuffi Raa was a pacifist, Lando installed a pair of auxiliary pedals beneath the cockpit's control console that allowed him to operate a pair of smaller laser weapons on the upper hull. Whenever he stepped outside his ship, he carried a remote-control device that enabled him to trigger all of the weapons, and also

carried a transponder that kept the *Falcon*'s guns from sweeping within a couple of degrees of whoever wore it.

When Han Solo obtained the *Falcon*, he and Chewbacca removed the auxiliary pedals because Solo found the foot-operated devices awkward, and the Wookiee needed the extra legroom. Anticipating that they would need to control the *Falcon*'s cannons from the cockpit, they installed a pair of trackball controllers to the left of the control console's central display monitor, and installed similar controls at the engineering stations. While the remote-control devices offer definite advantages, the one drawback is diminished accuracy with the cannons. Fortunately, the *Falcon* evades most attacks by way of stealth and sheer speed.

⬆⬆ Seated in the *Falcon*'s dorsal cannon turret, Han Solo wears a headset comlink so he can maintain communication with Chewbacca in the cockpit.

⬆ Protected by military-grade deflector shields, the cannon turrets' transparisteel windows offer clear views outside the ship. A single blast from the modified cannons can destroy a TIE fighter.

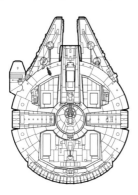

RETRACTABLE BLASTER CANNON

Although the mere sight of the *Millennium Falcon*'s large quad laser cannons can serve as a deterrent against enemy ships with lesser firepower, there is a distinct advantage in also having a weapon that the enemy *can't* see. To discourage sneak attacks while the *Falcon* is grounded, Han Solo installed an Ax-108 'Ground Buzzer' surface-defense blaster cannon that retracts into a concealed compartment beneath the ship's hull.

Manufactured by BlasTech, the Ground Buzzer is a semi-automatic anti-personnel weapon with a rate of fire of 12 energy-bursts per second. It can be operated manually from the cockpit or by a hand-held remote, or automatically via the ship's computer, and has a range of settings from stunning charges to armor-piercing capability. The Ground Buzzer is programmed not to fire at the *Falcon*'s crew or allied forces, or to hit any part of the *Falcon*, including her landing legs. Targeting sensors seek out energy signatures from enemy weapons, and a built-in computer determines which targets pose the most immediate threat before opening fire. A dedicated generator ensures the Ground Buzzer will operate even if the *Falcon*'s other electrical systems are shut down or have been temporarily disabled.

➔ During the Battle of Hoth, the *Falcon*'s Ground Buzzer's targeting computer assessed Imperial snowtroopers as unfriendly forces and provided lethal and suppressive fire while Han Solo prepared for lift-off.

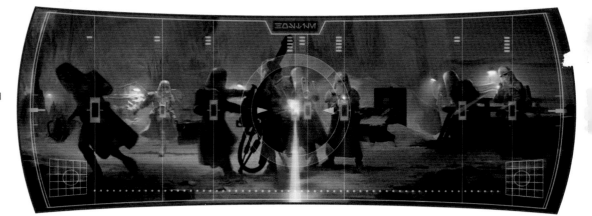

GROUND BUZZER

❶ Hydraulic swivel mount
❷ Power cables
❸ Large-capacity gas chamber
❹ Flexible gas hose
❺ Gas conversion enabler
❻ Actuating module
❼ Generator
❽ Built-in computer
❾ Targeting sensors
❿ Ventilated barrel housing
⓫ Emitter nozzle

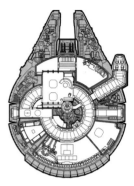

CONCUSSION MISSILES

Self-contained projectile weapons, concussion missiles are armed with explosive warheads and travel at sublight speeds. Designed for bombing attacks in atmospheres, where the concussion blast can cause tremendous devastation, the missiles have homing sensors that are very effective against stationary and slow-moving targets. They are also highly effective for outer-space combat.

The concussion missile's armored tube carries the warhead, a guidance computer, and a propellant system. Exterior shield projectors envelop the missile in an energy shield. Like proton torpedoes, concussion missiles can deliver a very powerful warhead to an energy-shielded target, but share the same disadvantage of being short-range weapons, with a maximum range of 700m.

Concussion missiles are normally fired in staggered pairs, with the second missile launching a fraction of a second after the first. The first missile penetrates the target's energy shields, then detonates to eliminate defensive shield generators and armor plating. A fraction of a second later, the second missile reaches the now-vulnerable target and inflicts maximum

damage. In atmospheres, a concussion warhead produces sonic booms and devastating ground tremors. In space combat, concussion missiles normally are used to destroy a capital ship's shield generators, allowing turbolasers to fire upon the target vessel. Under Imperial law it is illegal for a civilian to possess concussion missiles or launchers.

Han Solo armed the *Millennium Falcon* with a pair of Arakyd concussion missile launchers, and modified each launcher to carry up to four missiles from a variety of manufacturers, including Arakyd and Dymek. The standard missiles are Arakyd ST2 missiles, each more than a meter long, and as powerful as a standard proton torpedo. Concussion missile systems are easier to maintain than proton torpedo launchers, but they are hardly inexpensive, as each Arakyd ST2 missile costs approximately 750 credits.

The *Falcon*'s target-acquiring sensors send data directly to the missiles' built-in guidance computers. When Lando Calrissian piloted the *Falcon* into the second Death Star's reactor, he fired a pair of Arakyd ST2 concussion missiles that helped destroy the Imperial battle station.

ARAKYD ST2 CONCUSSION MISSILE

OPTIMUM RANGE: **300M**

MAXIMUM RANGE: **700M**

❶ Stabilizer fin

❷ Exhaust nozzle

❸ Propellant chamber

❹ Energy envelope projector

❺ Concussion cylinder

❻ Armor-piercing warhead

DYMEK CONCUSSION MISSILE

OPTIMUM RANGE: **260M**

MAXIMUM RANGE: **750M**

❶ Exhaust nozzle

❷ Energy envelope projector

❸ Streamlined concussion chamber

❹ Armor-piercing warhead

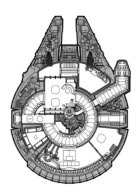

DEFLECTOR SHIELDING

Vital to survival aboard nearly every starship, deflector shields surround a ship in protective force fields. A deflector shield generator, the shield's power source, determines the shield's strength, radius, and also the amount of damage it can absorb. Deflector shields are projected just a few molecules underneath hull plating, but different power settings and configurations can extend a shield farther away from the hull. Smaller ships, such as starfighters, are typically equipped with a single deflector shield generator that can be adjusted and directed to protect specific parts of the vessel, while larger ships have multiple deflector shield generators dedicated to different areas.

There are two types of deflector shields: particle shielding and ray shielding. Particle shielding repels solid objects such as space debris and high-velocity projectiles. Because particle shielding completely surrounds a ship, it must be temporarily turned off before a ship can fire its own missile, launch an escape pod, or receive a shuttlecraft.

Ray shielding, also known as energy shielding, protects against stellar and magnetic radiation, lasers, blasters, and other energy beams. Ray shielding does not stop solid matter. Because large amounts of energy are required to maintain ray shielding, ships equipped with ray-shield generators typically set the shields at a low-energy level as a standard defense against radiation, and increase power to the shields as a defense against enemy fire.

Although both types of shielding are needed for complete protection, the Empire restricted the use of high-energy ray shielding to gain a tactical advantage over most private and commercial vessels in Imperial space. Non-Imperial vessels were required to apply for permits to carry ray shielding, but the standard explanation of 'fear of piracy' was usually sufficient to secure permission.

Han Solo refuses to discuss details, but rumor has it that he 'acquired' several military-grade deflector shield generators from the Imperial maintenance facilities on Myomar. The *Millennium Falcon*'s

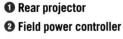

❶ **Rear projector**
❷ **Field power controller**
❸ **Over-charge emitter**
❹ **Navigational deflector**
❺ **Main forward projector**
❻ **Particle neutralizer**
❼ **Energizer**
❽ **Polarizer**
❾ **Ion isolator**
❿ **Ion collectors**

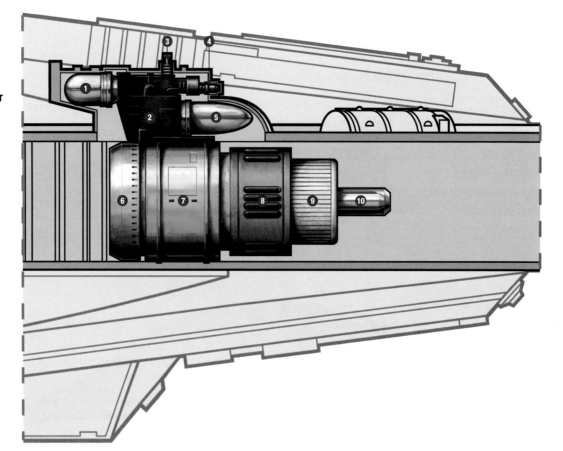

deflector shield generators include a Torplex shield generator and a Nordoxicon anti-concussion field generator to protect the ship's forward areas. The Torplex generator is supported by a Novaldex stasis-type shield generator that feeds port and starboard projectors. The Novaldex is part of the crucial system that prevents passengers and cargoes from aging at a dramatically different rate than 'realspace time' while traveling at faster-than-light speeds.

A military-grade Kuat Drive Yard (KDY) deflector shield generator protects the aft. An additional navigational deflector system mounted between the ship's forward mandibles normally keeps space ahead clear of small to microscopic impact debris. The *Falcon*'s shields are maneuverable and can be angled to combine energy against enemy fire from a specific direction, ensuring deflector power is available whether the *Falcon* is engaged in frontal attack or full retreat.

The *Falcon* is equipped with exotic reactant-impeller units that serve the engines as well as the deflector shields. Working in conjunction with a Koensayr TLB power converter, the reactant-impeller units enable the shields to absorb enemy fire and feed that energy directly into the Quadex power core; this energy can be in turn re-routed to the *Falcon*'s engines and weaponry. While these shielding systems allow the *Falcon* to withstand heavy attacks, it must be noted that the *Falcon* can endure such abuse for limited duration only, as the ship's engines are not designed to provide the incredible power necessary to run military-grade shields continuously.

GRAVITY FIELD STABILIZER AND COMPENSATOR

Because most spacefaring species are susceptible to the forces of gravity, a KapriCorp acceleration compensator enables the *Falcon*'s crew to move about within the ship as well as carry out high-speed maneuvers without being pulverized by gravitational forces. When landing on high- or low-gravity worlds, the *Falcon*'s gravity flux stabilizer automatically adjusts to maintain a consistent intensity of gravity within the ship.

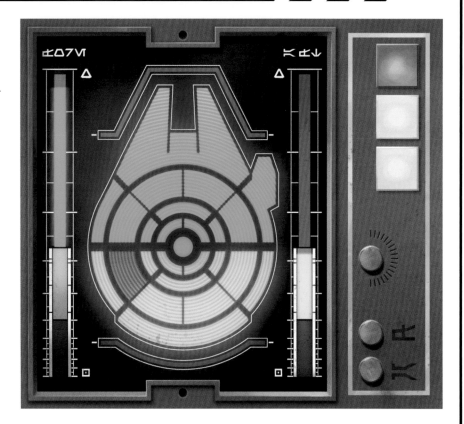

Shields are holding at an optimal power level

All shield power is routed to the forward section for extra strength but the aft is left vulnerable

All shield power is routed to the aft section. This option is typically only used in rare atmospheric circumstances. It is not recommended during space flight as micrometeorites would be extremely damaging during forward acceleration

Yellow indicates shield strength is failing

Shield quadrants under attack will blink red. Solid red indicates the shields have failed

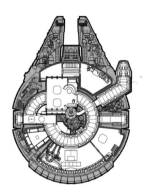

TRACTOR BEAM PROJECTOR

Also known informally as a grappling ray or magnetic beam, a tractor beam is a powerful, invisible, and maneuverable force field that, when projected into space, can snare, shift, or redirect objects. The force field is produced by a tractor beam generator, then released by a tractor beam projector. Spaceports and docking bays rely upon short-range tractor beams and simple targeting systems for traffic control, and help guide ships for safe landings and departures. Tractor beams are common armaments aboard military vessels, which use incredibly strong beams that are capable of capturing small ships in mid-flight, but this is not always an easy task. Targeting fast and maneuverable craft can be a challenge for even the most advanced tractor beam systems.

Freighters and container ships generally use commercial tractor beams to move cargo modules as well as for docking procedures. The *Millennium Falcon* is equipped with a pair of Phylon C5 tractor beam emitters mounted in opposing positions beside the freight-loading arms within the forward mandibles. Operated from the cockpit, engineering stations, or control console in the freight-loading room, the tractor beam has a rated range of 30m and can easily lift up to 900kg.

Like most commercial tractor beam technology, the Phylon C5 units are not suited for military purpose because of their short-range and simple targeting systems, and they are not powerful enough to snare a fast and maneuverable enemy craft. However, Chewbacca has become such an expert with tractor beam controls that he can rescue falling bodies.

❶ **Main beam emitter**
❷ **Control pulse emitters**
❸ **Polarization multiplier**
❹ **Circuit access**
❺ **Generator housing**
❻ **Primary matter coils**
❼ **Field dispersion inhibitors**
❽ **Counter-rotating field assemblies**
❾ **Generator control module**
❿ **Maintenance override**
⓫ **Power and control input**
⓬ **Primary focusing rings**

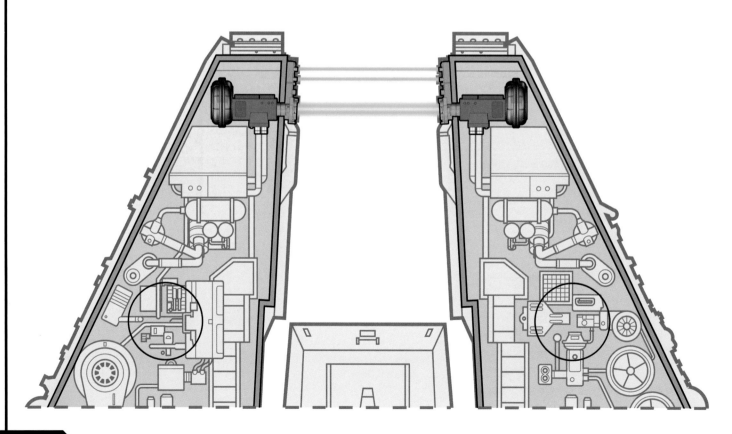

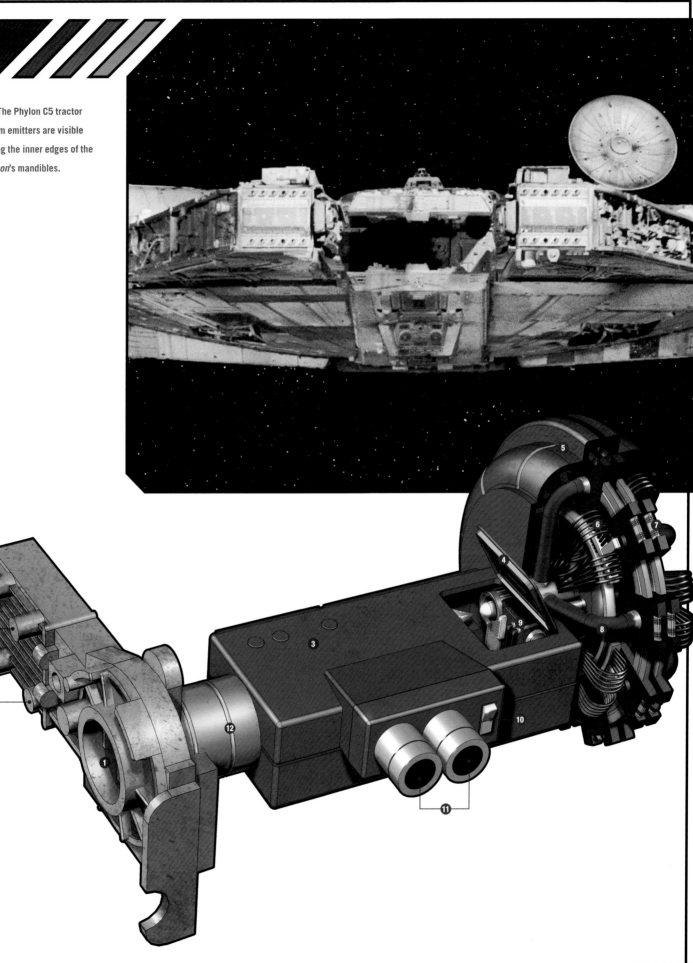

→ The Phylon C5 tractor beam emitters are visible along the inner edges of the *Falcon*'s mandibles.

Rusted, dingy, dented by micrometeoroids, and carbon-scored by laser fire, the *Millennium Falcon*'s battered exterior looks like a tramp freighter on her last legs, and suggests a total lack of care on the owner's part. Like previous owners of the *Falcon*, Han Solo does not bother to conceal the hammered-out dents, durasteel-patched breaches, or epoxatal-filled cracks, and he leaves most of the rust as is. In fact, the *Falcon*'s appearance has been a deliberate deception ever since she became the property of smugglers. Han Solo and Chewbacca know that pirates, thieves, and Imperial Customs agents are less attracted to a ship that looks as if she's ready for the scrapyard, and they do everything they can to maintain the *Falcon*'s dilapidated appearance. This apparent disregard of the *Falcon*'s exterior also allows her crew to focus time and money on adding new technology, modifying and upgrading her systems, and maintaining her engines.

Despite appearances, the *Falcon*'s hull is actually in remarkably good shape. Solo and Chewbacca have fused and welded sheets of scavenged duralloy plating over the most vital areas of the hull, providing warship-grade protection for its engines and crew compartments. Much of the plating came from the Imperial derelict *Liquidator*, a *Neutron Star*-class bulk cruiser that was a casualty of the Battle of Nar Shaddaa. The combination of duralloy plating and military-grade energy-shielding systems ensures that the *Falcon* is almost impervious to standard laser weapons, and can take a severe pounding with minimal damage before she either returns fire or escapes into hyperspace.

← The *Millennium Falcon*'s battle-scarred hull is a testament to her durability and violent past.

1 Military-grade armor
2 Interlocking edges
3 Impact damage
4 Mismatched plate
5 Carbon scoring
6 Durasteel plate
7 Duralloy welds
8 Reinforced frame

YT-1300 ENGINEERING SYSTEMS

From the
CEC YT-1300 Buyers' Guide

orellian Engineering Corporation knows that time equals credits, and that not every YT-1300 crew will include a captain, pilot, co-pilot, astronavigator, communications systems operator, engineer, technician, gunner, and operations manager. That's why we designed the YT-1300 to be operated by a crew of two, and provide every buyer with clear instructions and guidelines for maintaining and controlling the ship's engineering systems.

The YT-1300 holds a Quadex power core, the most powerful energy core currently available to the commercial market. The Quadex provides power for the Girodyne SRB42 sublight engines and Isu-Sim SSP05 hyperdrive. All of the engineering controls are conveniently located in the YT-1300's aft engine room, and have been designed for ease of use by most spacefaring, dexterous life forms. With proper care and routine maintenance, these energy and propulsion systems should provide many years of trouble-free operation.

Holding a fusioncutter, Chewbacca stands in a maintenance bay below the deck of the *Millennium Falcon*'s main hold to access components related to the hyperdrive.

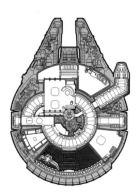

Given that Han Solo's tinkering amounts to the *Millennium Falcon* being in a constant state of modification, the ship operates surprisingly well. This would not be possible if Solo did not update and monitor each modification by way of the ship's technical and engineering stations.

The largest chamber in the *Millennium Falcon*, the engine room contains the ship's most vital systems: the sublight engines, the hyperdrive, and a diagnostic terminal for the engines. These systems are extensively jury-rigged, with extra cables and conduits that connect everything in an elaborate maze of technology. A console displays data from the centralized system that monitors and controls machinery throughout

the ship. The engine room also contains the main switchboard for control and distribution of energy on board. A small section of the engine room is dedicated to the *Falcon*'s 'library' of datacards, which include technical manuals and files for maintenance management.

A freight elevator built into the engine room's floor allows cargo to be brought up from below. Five individual sections of deck plating can be removed to access the *Falcon*'s single-passenger escape pods. To help prevent accidents to either controls or cargo within the engine room, cargo is generally transferred to a different hold, but it can also be secured to the deck.

❶ **Telescoping lift system**
❷ **Retractable pressure doors**
❸ **Cargo**
❹ **Hydraulic lift drives**
❺ **Adjustable gravity field plating**
❻ **Loading ramp**

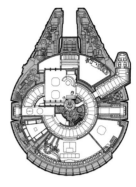

Before Lando Calrissian acquired the *Millennium Falcon*, a previous owner modified the engineering station located in a nook within the ship's circular corridor. This station is primarily dedicated to regulating the flow of energy from the modified Quadex power core, but also allows the crew to monitor and adjust controls for the engine room without actually entering it. In the 'stock' YT-1300, a protective access panel covered this station and its delicate console; the panel is long gone, but Han Solo and Chewbacca prefer the station to be easily accessible.

An adjustable swivel-mounted seat is positioned before the station, but the seat is easily removable and the station's components can be elevated for operators who prefer to stand. Controls for upgraded engine-cooling units and ventilation systems, as well as extant smoke damage on the engine room's ceiling and bulkheads, suggest that the auxiliary station may have been installed after a fire in the engine room, or because the engines had once generated an excessive amount of heat.

Han Solo's modifications to the engineering station include the installation of a manual attach/release mechanism for the *Falcon*'s landing claw. This allows Solo and Chewbacca to secure and release the *Falcon* to and from natural or artificial surfaces without emitting energy that might be intercepted by foreign sensors.

❶ **Hyperdrive status monitor**
❷ **Emergency hyperdrive shutdown**
❸ **Temperature gauge**
❹ **Engine-cooling controls**
❺ **Quadex power core controls**
❻ **Data input**
❼ **Power core monitor**
❽ **Ventilation controls**
❾ **Manual controls for landing claw**
❿ **Data monitor**
⓫ **Keypad**
⓬ **Strongbox containing astrogation plotter and chart for emergencies**

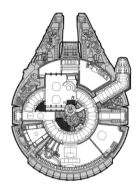

↓ **C-3PO stands before the engineering station in the** *Millennium Falcon***'s main hold.**

TECHNICAL STATION

Inside the *Millennium Falcon*'s main hold, a previous owner's sleeping alcove was removed to accommodate a technical station, which Han Solo uses to monitor his many improvements to the *Falcon*. The station consists of a large Fabritech ANq-51 sensor array computer terminal, salvaged from an aging Corellian corvette, that stores sensor and navigational data, and serves this data to the ship's droid brains. A portion of the adjoining bulkhead contains circuitry that connects the engineering station to both the Rubicon navicomputer and the Isu-Sim hyperdrive engine.

CIRCUITRY BAYS

The *Millennium Falcon* holds two circuitry bays. The first one, situated near the ship's power core, was a standard feature for every stock YT-1300 configuration. This bay offers maintenance access to all essential power distribution systems, and has a removable floor section to provide access to the lower systems.

An unidentified previous owner, who may have been more interested in technical proficiency than lost cargo space, added the second circuitry bay to allow for easier access to the *Falcon*'s power conduits and backup systems. This circuitry bay

opens directly into the main hold, and can also be accessed through a secondary hatch from the port-side corridor. The floor is partly recessed for access to the lower systems.

Both circuitry bays are linked and have automatic shut-down controls in case one is damaged or malfunctions. During a period when Solo and Chewbacca were operating in the Corporate Sector, some of the *Falcon*'s control circuitry was damaged. Limited options forced them to temporarily utilize adaptor fittings and interface routers to use gas and liquid fluidic components until they could replace the inferior technology with shielded circuits.

❶ **Ship status indicator**
❷ **Power distribution adjusters**
❸ **Indicator lights**
❹ **Data input/diagnostic ports**
❺ **Missing access panel**

❻ **Circuit access**
❼ **Lighting**
❽ **Static charge dissipator**
❾ **Air-cooling intake**
❿ **Expansion plates**

⓫ **Electrical systems panel**
⓬ **Life-support systems**
⓭ **Gravity compensator**
⓮ **Maintenance opening**
⓯ **Sensor relays**

↑ Princess Leia Organa makes repairs inside the *Falcon*'s circuitry bay.

HANX-WARGEL COMPUTER

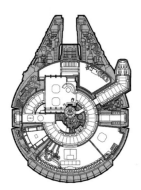

Starships require at least one main computer to manage all the ship's systems, including sensors, navigation, and propulsion. In her original stock configuration, the *Millennium Falcon* was equipped with a Hanx-Wargel SuperFlow IV computer, a 'new generation' of droid brain that supervised the YT-1300's powerful sublight and hyperspace engines. The Hanx-Wargel was considered highly sophisticated and extremely flexible, qualities that enabled it easily to manage modified and retrofitted systems.

The *Falcon*'s computer has been torn down and rebuilt more than once over the years. According to the *Falcon*'s records, the original Hanx-Wargel droid brain was replaced by an amalgam of a targeting and fire-control brain that may have been salvaged from a Separatist vessel following the Clone Wars. The Hanx-Wargel currently contains three separate and distinct droid brains as slave computers and extra memory. The droid brains were cannibalized from a military-issue R3 astromech, a V-5 transport droid, and a corporate espionage slicer droid. Although the three droid brains generally work well together during emergencies, they bicker constantly when not fully employed with more important duties.

Some mechanics have described the *Falcon*'s Hanx-Wargel as an abomination, and have expressed astonishment that the computer manages the myriad of melded, jury-rigged and modified systems. However, a few mechanics have attempted to replicate the computer for other ships in efforts to achieve greater efficiency and speed. All such efforts have ended disastrously.

❶ Original Hanx-Wargel brain
❷ Primary interconnect couplings
❸ Environmental sub-processor
❹ Propulsion sub-processor
❺ Diagnostic interface
❻ Navigation sub-processor
❼ Communication sub-processor
❽ Slicer droid brain
❾ R3 astromech brain
❿ V-5 transport droid brain

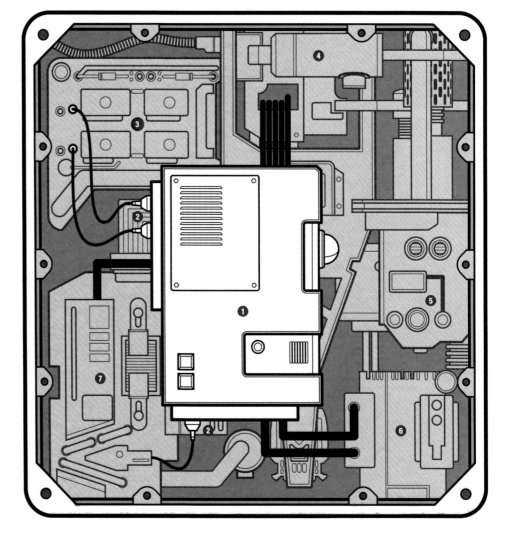

→ R2-D2 interfaces with the *Millennium Falcon*'s computer to reactivate the disabled hyperdrive.

8

9

10

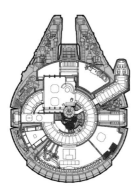

Like most starships, the YT-1300 uses a fusion system that contains a hypermatter-annihilation core, or power core. The *Millennium Falcon*'s Quadex power core provides power for the hyperdrive generator, and is much more powerful than the portable chemical, fission, and fusion reactors used for domestic devices. A progressive combustion reaction power converter, located in the number three hold, routes energy from the Quadex power core to the *Falcon*'s propulsion units.

Because the Quadex is essentially what keeps the entire ship running, it is housed within the YT-1300's central hub, the most protected area. Although the Quadex has been modified to accommodate numerous customizations, such as feeding power directly to the *Falcon*'s AG-2G quad laser cannons, its general appearance is similar to when it was brand new. A closer inspection yields the fact that the *Falcon*'s Quadex was completely retooled long before Lando Calrissian acquired the ship.

❶ Condenser

❷ Pressure convection driver

❸ Primary reactor vessel

❹ Reactor core

❺ Auxiliary power port

❻ Primary heat exchanger

❼ Flow regulators

❽ Thermal regulator

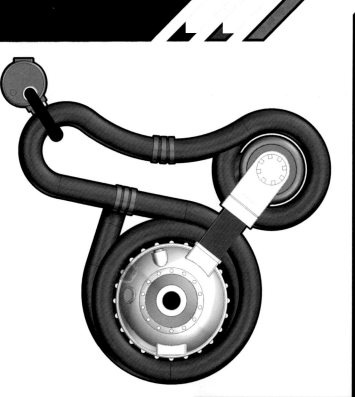

MYNOCKS

A common pest to travelers throughout the galaxy, mynocks are leathery-winged, parasitic creatures that survive in the vacuum of space. Mynocks are nourished by stellar radiation, but also feed on silica and other minerals. Mynocks travel in packs and typically grow to be 1.6m long from head to tail, with a wingspan of approximately 1.25m. A bristly suction-cup-like mouth enables them to affix themselves to passing starships and chew on power cables, to which they are partial. Because damage to any power cables can be disastrous, pilots must routinely inspect their ships for mynock infestations.

Although exposure to certain atmospheric gases as well as planetary gravity can be deadly to mynocks, they can survive and breed on planets too. To prevent problems with mynocks, most planetary spaceports scan incoming ships for evidence of mynocks, and require freighter pilots to shake off the creatures before landing, as failure to do so typically violates planetary quarantine protocols. Blaster weapons or concentrated bursts of superheated vapor are generally sufficient methods for removing mynocks from starship hulls.

➜ Illuminated by the *Millennium Falcon*'s floodlights, a mynock attempts to absorb energy through the suction-cup-like mouth located between its eye stalks.

YT-1300 SENSORS

From the
CEC YT-1300 Buyers' Guide

As most spacefarers know, the term 'sensors' covers a wide range of devices used to detect and analyze data. While simple sensor devices such as hand-held macrobinoculars—which gather and enhance visual data—and short-range radiation detectors are useful for planetary expeditions, more sophisticated sensors are required for space travel. Such sensors include devices used to collect and analyze data about light, radio, and other electromagnetic emissions; sound, motion, and vibration; gravitational, nuclear, and magnetic fields; heat, pressure, and trace chemicals; and even other sensors.

Corellian Engineering Corporation has outfitted the YT-1300 with a sensor suite perfectly suited for navigation, collision avoidance, research, and exploration. While this sensor suite is suitable for travel between many worlds in the Galactic Core, owners of merchant ships with routes in the outlying systems, where piracy may pose a threat, should consider purchasing additional CEC-authorized sensors as an added measure of precaution.

Although literally thousands of different sensors are available on the commercial market, CEC acknowledges that no sensor is entirely perfect. Solar radiation, hydrogen clouds, asteroid fields, strong gravity wells, and other natural phenomena can cause interference or block sensors, and deliberate jamming or concealment can hide things from even the most sophisticated sensors. While CEC cannot guarantee that sensors are the solution to evade every obstacle, experienced travelers will verify that a diverse sensor array is crucial to surviving the myriad challenges of space travel.

⇐ The *Millennium Falcon*'s large sensor rectenna is her most prominent sensor apparatus, but sophisticated sensor technology is distributed throughout the ship.

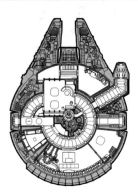

In sensor technology, there are essentially two sensor modes: active and passive. Active sensors—also known as scan-mode sensors—emit controlled bursts of energy to detect and collect the reflected energy as it 'bounces' off bodies within the sensors' range. Passive sensors, such as heat detectors and simple telescopes, detect energy emitted by other sources. Although sensors are absolutely necessary for space travel, pilots should be aware that sensor-radiated energy is generally 'visible' to other ships' sensors. Relatively, active sensors emit energy that can be easily detected, while passive sensors require less energy and are usually more difficult to detect.

To function properly, a typical sensor array requires three components: a long-range sensor that can scan the area around the starship and collect data; a computer to evaluate the collected data; and a display to present the computer's findings in text, graphics, or holographic images. Because larger ships generally have room for larger computers and more attachment points for specialized sensors, large vessels can sometimes have a tactical advantage. However, pilots should note that large vessels also radiate more energy, reflect more light, cause more gravitational disturbances, and can be regarded as bigger targets.

The *Millennium Falcon*'s sensor suite is a powerful, compact military package that was originally built for long-range scout ships. The package includes full-spectrum transceivers (FSTs), which are also known

1. **Range markings**
2. **Spatial grid**
3. **Hostile contact**
4. **Gas pocket**
5. **Impact threat zone**
6. **Shield range**
7. **Active sector**
8. **Inanimate debris**

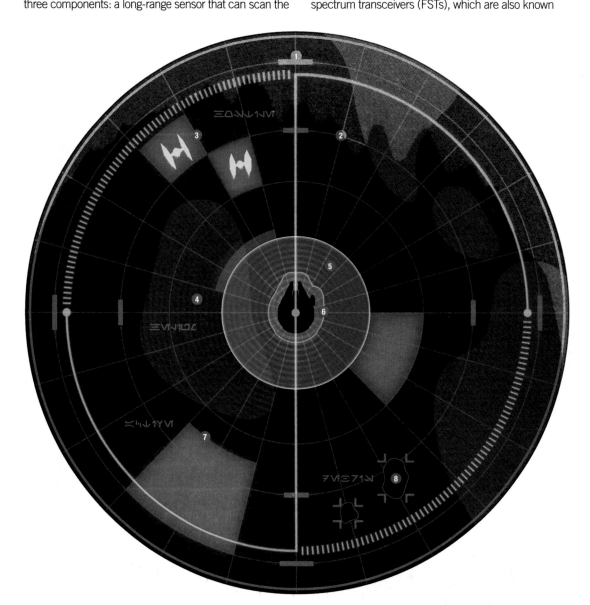

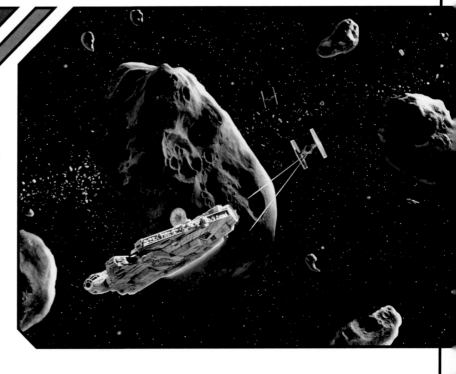

as 'universal sensors' because they use a variety of scanners to detect all types of objects, energy, and fields. The size of the *Falcon*'s receptor dish not only increases the accuracy of detecting objects at long range but also increases the range of the powerful electro-photo receptor (EPR), which is crucial for the *Falcon*'s targeting sensors, and the subspace comm detector.

The *Falcon*'s sensor suite includes dedicated energy receptors (DERs), which detect any electromagnetic emission within range of the sensor array, including comlink transmissions, navigational beacons, heat, and laser light. DERs are the primary passive sensor device in military sensor arrays, and are illegal for nearly all non-military ships.

SENSOR SWEEPS

Extremely effective at short and medium range, active sensors 'sweep' areas of space to gather data. There are three different prime modes of sensor sweep: *scan, search,* and *focus.*

In scan mode, sensors look at everything around the entire vessel. Either slow and thorough, or swift and perfunctory, scan mode provides basic information about the environment outside the ship, such as whether and how many other ships are in the area. If the scans yield any potential hazards, a warning indicator will notify the pilot and direct attention to the perceived threat.

In search mode, sensors only look for a specific type of target, such as a ship or radioactive frequency. The pilot or sensor operator must indicate the type of target before conducting the search.

When a number of ships travel in formation across space, pilots often 'search' their sensors on overlapping areas; the lead pilot typically focuses sensors directly ahead while other pilots focus their sensors to the sides and behind. When used in conjunction with a navicomputer, search mode can help plot emergency routes to evade enemy ships or asteroid belts.

In focus mode, sensors are concentrated on a particular area selected by the pilot. This tight focus yields more detailed information about the targeted area, but little or nothing is detected outside this area. Focus mode is often used once something 'unusual' has been detected by more general sensor sweeps.

⬅ Sensor waves radiate out from the Siep-Irol passive sensor antennas in the *Falcon*'s mandibles. The receptor dish is typically directed forward in flight, but it can be repositioned for focused scans of specific areas.

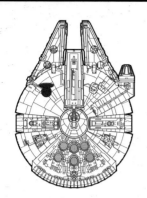

Most of the *Millennium Falcon*'s sensor and communications systems are located in the ship's military-grade rectenna, which is mounted dorsally on the port bow, but backup systems are emplaced throughout the hull. The rectenna dish is controlled by a Fabritech ANq-51 sensor array computer and includes a power-boosted electro-photo receptor, active and passive long-range sensor arrays, and a subspace communications detector. Short-range target-acquisition programs also can be patched into the dish.

The electro-photo receptor (EPR) is a simple sensor that combines data from sophisticated normal light, ultraviolet, and infrared telescopes to form a composite two-dimensional picture on the *Falcon*'s datascreens. The EPR works in conjunction with the *Falcon*'s targeting sensors to transmit images of targets for display on monitors in the cockpit and gun turrets.

A Fabritech ANy-20 active sensor transceiver and a Siep-Irol passive sensor antenna are built into the *Falcon*'s mandibles. Although Fabritech and Siep-Irol devices are not generally compatible, Solo modified the passive sensor array and rigged the *Falcon*'s computer to read it as a Fabritech-friendly unit. The *Falcon*'s subspace comm detector scans for transmissions from other ships and nearby planets.

The *Falcon*'s communications system is less sophisticated than her sensors, but it includes a powerful jamming program. The onboard Carbanti signal-augmented sensor jammer masks the YT-1300 behind a screen of static, random signals, or false responses, and can also block transmissions from nearby vessels. A significant drawback to any jammer is that while it may conceal a ship's exact position in space, the jammer also emits energy that effectively broadcasts the ship's general location to other vessels' sensors. To gain a tactical advantage, Solo has linked his jammer with a Carbanti 29L electro-

↑ A TIE fighter makes a close pass over the *Falcon*'s rectenna dish.

➜ A standard CEC civilian model sensor dish designed for the YT series compared to the larger, military-grade rectenna mounted on the *Falcon*.

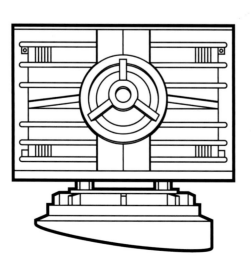

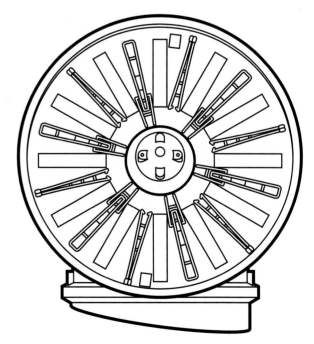

magnetic countermeasures package to expand and scatter the jammer's broadcast, making it more difficult for enemy ships to pinpoint the *Falcon*'s position.

Despite Solo's inventive handiwork, the *Falcon*'s jamming system is not entirely foolproof. The first time it was used, it generated such a powerful pulse that it jammed the *Falcon*'s own internal communications, disrupting signals from the cockpit to the ship's systems. Fortunately the jammer burned out, allowing Solo and Chewbacca to regain control of the ship. Chewbacca claims the jamming system's flaws were corrected, but Solo remains cautious of activating the jammer unless it's absolutely necessary.

❶ Attitude adjust servo
❷ Electro-magnetic
   countermeasures package
❸ Demodulation processor
❹ Reflector elements
❺ Multi-element transmitter array
❻ Photo receptor node
❼ Subspace comm detector
❽ Sensor jammer array

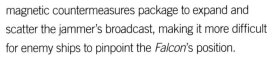

FABRITECH

A leading manufacturer of sensors and communications devices for nearly a century, Fabritech produces everything from handheld comlinks to starship sensor suites. Headquartered on the planet Fabrin, the company's primary design goal is durability. All Fabritech devices are engineered to function in a variety of harsh environments, from searing desert worlds to water and ice planets. Both the Empire and Rebel Alliance relied on Fabritech gear throughout the Galactic Civil War.

TOPOGRAPHIC SENSORS

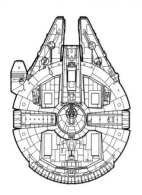

The *Millennium Falcon*'s sensor suite includes special terrain following sensors (TFS), which utilize a combination of sophisticated sonic, optical, and radiation sensors to create detailed topographic displays on the *Falcon*'s datascreens. Originally developed for scout ships, the TFS can cut through everything from dense cloud cover to forest canopies, searching for potential hazards and concealed landing areas, and 'paints' topographic displays in near-instantaneous time. Working in conjunction with the navicomputer, the TFS can help plot courses over treacherous areas of previously unmapped worlds as well as through densely settled urban environments.

The many uses for the TFS include finding clearings in jungle forests, large caverns on ice planets, and islands on rain-shrouded water worlds. The TFS also allows pilots to navigate through serpentine canyons and tunnels, or through total darkness. Whether the *Falcon*'s crew is looking for an impromptu hideout or the best route for a quick getaway, they frequently rely upon the TFS to provide the visual data they need to get the job done.

1 **Rebel base**
2 **Rebel Alliance coded beacon**
3 **Ancient temple**
4 **Dense jungle canopy**
5 **Terrain grid**
6 **Yavin IV**
7 **Surface data**
8 **Attitude indicator**
9 **Screen activator**
10 **Mode selectors**

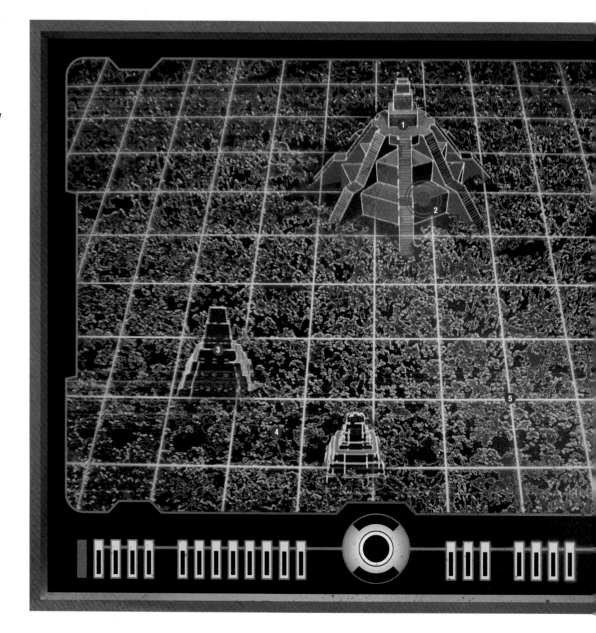

→ The topographic sensors map the dense jungle of Yavin IV to guide the *Falcon* to the Rebel base.

↘ Through the *Falcon*'s cockpit canopy, Han Solo views what appear to be rock formations inside a cavern, but quickly realizes the *Falcon* has traveled into the maw of an enormous space slug.

↘↘ As the space slug closes its jaws, Solo sees an opportunity for escape, and angles the *Falcon* to pass between the creature's massive teeth. Solo subsequently modified the terrain following sensors to recognize space slugs.

UNCHARTED TERRITORY

Following the Battle of Hoth, Han Solo guided the *Millennium Falcon* into an asteroid belt in an effort to evade four Imperial TIE fighters. Two fighters were destroyed almost immediately during the pursuit before Solo headed for a large planetoid that was covered by jagged rock formations. Using his daring and quick reflexes in combination with the *Falcon*'s terrain following sensors, Solo led the two remaining TIE fighters into a narrow passage between cliffs, from which only the *Falcon* emerged unscathed.

The terrain following sensors also determined that what appeared to be a nearby crater was really a deep cavern, an ideal place for Han to hide the *Falcon* before the inevitable arrival of more Imperial fighters. Unfortunately, the sensors failed to ascertain that the *Falcon* was actually entering the maw of an enormous life form. By the time Solo realized his error, he also knew that it would take more than sophisticated sensors to deliver the *Falcon* to safety.

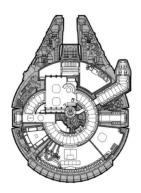

↓ The *Millennium Falcon*'s fake transponder codes prevent Imperial authorities from immediately identifying the YT-1300.

TRANSPONDER CODES

For thousands of years, the Bureau of Ships and Services (BoSS) has maintained and regulated data about nearly every ship in the civilized areas of the galaxy. To accomplish their goal and maintain up-to-date records, the BoSS equips every ship with an individual transponder code, a unique signal that is beamed out continuously to identify each vessel. This code includes the ship's name, type, owner, and other pertinent data, and is built into a ship's sublight engine. It is created by producing a slight variation in the frequency of the engine's emissions. This variation, as well as data about the ship, is encoded in the transponder director that is sealed into the engine itself.

Agents from BoSS are reputed to be incorruptible, but there are three ways to alter transponder codes. The easiest method is to replace a ship's sublight engines with engines from another ship, preferably one with a cleaner record. A second way is to install false transponder codes in the existing engine, so that when the modified ship is scanned it will be identified as a different vessel. Although this may sound easier than replacing the engine, installing false transponder codes is a complex procedure, requires expensive forgery technology, and—if the forgery attempt fails—may cause the transponder to melt the engine's internal components. The third method is to tamper with BoSS's files directly, which is extremely difficult because their codes are almost indecipherable.

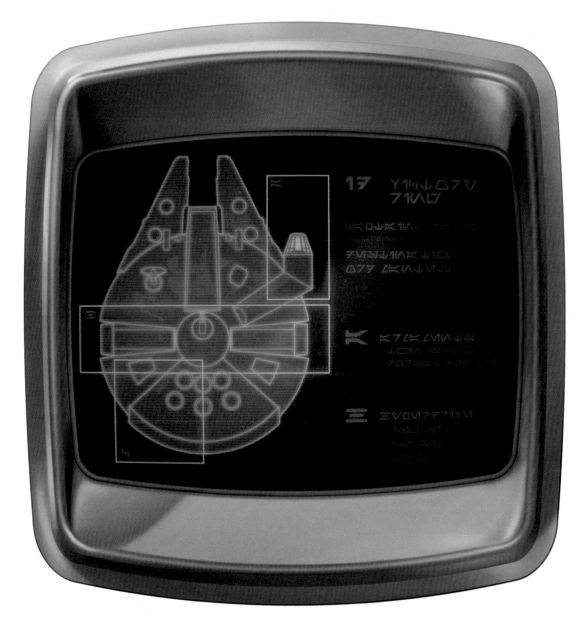

← An Imperial screen displaying one of the ship's many false identities, *Victory Ring*, during an incident on Ord Mantell.

IFF TRANSPONDER

Of all the *Millennium Falcon*'s illegal add-ons, the most audacious is an Imperial 'identify friend/foe' (IFF) transponder. Used extensively by the Imperial fleet, the IFF system enables military interrogation systems to distinguish allied vessels from enemies. Han Solo uses the illicit IFF transponder in combination with the *Falcon*'s long-range scanners as insurance against detection, as the transponder allows the *Falcon* to spot and identify distant ships several minutes before those ships are aware of the *Falcon*'s presence.

The IFF transponder also serves to disguise the *Falcon*'s identification profile. Solo and Chewbacca rigged the IFF transponder's identification code and broadcast signal so that the *Falcon* can appear on Imperial scanners as everything from a drone barge to an Imperial research vessel. Solo has registered the *Falcon* in hundreds of different ports under dozens of different names, and the ship's transponder is programmed to broadcast several identity codes. The *Falcon*'s known aliases include the *Sunfighter Franchise*, *Close Shave*, and *Victory Ring*.

CREW FACILITIES

From the
CEC YT-1300 Buyers' Guide

Corellian Engineering Corporation knows that customer satisfaction goes far beyond whether the pilot's seat is comfortable and the controls are in reach. CEC also knows that no two customers are exactly the same. While other starship manufacturers typically limit crew-facilities options to humanoid customers, CEC builds ships for *all* spacefarers.

CEC takes pride in providing the best options for every YT-1300 owner, and offers a wide selection of crew-facilities modules for individual requirements. Whether an owner wants utilitarian quarters with an economical sleeping pallet or a luxury cabin with a transparisteel viewport fit for a shipping magnate, CEC crew-facilities modules are available for every preference and budget.

The stock YT-1300 has cabins linked by curved passage tubes. Padded to protect crew and passengers, the passage tubes provide sufficient clearance for many life forms up to two meters in height, and are wide enough to accommodate standard cargo containers. Although smaller passage tubes are available, and are frequently requested by relatively diminutive crews to effectively increase their freighter's cargo capacity, all YT-1300 owners should be aware that most commercial regions require freighters to be accessible to customs officers. CEC recommends you contact your local Space Ministry and law-enforcement authorities to confirm whether smaller passage tubes are legal in the areas you choose to travel.

For crew quarters, modules typically have built-in bunks, seats, tables, and storage compartments. To conserve space, many furnishings are designed to fold flat or retract into bulkheads or the deck. Refresher-closet or full-bath modules can be integrated with crew quarters or installed in separate locations. All modules come with built-in lighting components, and can be easily wired to the freighter's electrical systems.

As for recreation, CEC offers entertainment consoles and tables that are compatible with the most popular media and gaming systems. Whether you enjoy watching inflight holovids, playing grav-pool, listening to music, or physical exercise during a long journey through hyperspace, you'll enjoy your downtime that much more on your well-equipped YT-1300.

Before ordering your YT-1300, CEC recommends you contact an authorized CEC dealer to discuss your needs and expectations. If you purchase a previously owned YT-1300 and find any aspect of the freighter does not meet your requirements, a CEC representative can explain your modification and upgrade options.

⬅ R2-D2 stands beside the crew's lounge area in the *Millennium Falcon*'s main hold.

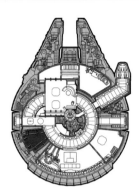

When Han Solo and Chewbacca obtained the *Millennium Falcon*, the captain's quarters consisted of a cramped cubicle that contained a sleeping pallet lined with free-fall netting that hung from retainers in a bulkhead, a tiny desk and chair, and a minuscule closet. They removed a bulkhead to expand this cubicle, creating quarters that hold three bunks, additional storage compartments, and a refresher closet. The larger storage compartments contain Solo's wardrobe. A single shelf is reserved for Chewbacca's comb.

Because of their hazardous line of work, Solo felt compelled to add a mediscan unit to one of the bunks. Most of the mediscan apparatus was scavenged from a late-model Athakam II Med Unit (the slang term is a 'med bed'), including articulated robotic limbs, a small display, and an input panel. Like a bioscan, the mediscan surveys an individual's biological make-up, origin, age, and other factors, and relies on both hardware and software to detect anomalies and health problems. While less capable than a full sickbay, the mediscan can diagnose and treat injuries ranging from blaster burns to deep flesh wounds.

➜ Inside the *Falcon's* crew quarters, Princess Leia uses emergency medical equipment to treat Luke Skywalker's injuries after his duel with Darth Vader.

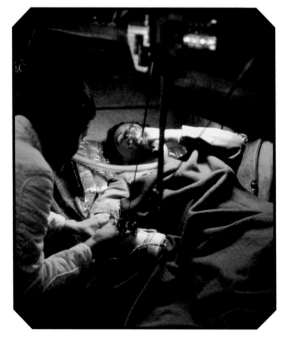

1 **Hanging bar**
2 **Closet**
3 **Storage lockers**
4 **Bunk comfort controls**
5 **Modified medical bunk**
6 **Refresher**
7 **Hatch**
8 **Hatch guide rails**
9 **Equipment cases**
10 **Bunks (3)**
11 **Floor grate**
12 **Drawers**
13 **Sonic shower**
14 **Corridor ring padding**
15 **Floor guide lights**
16 **Main corridor**
17 **Reinforced framework**

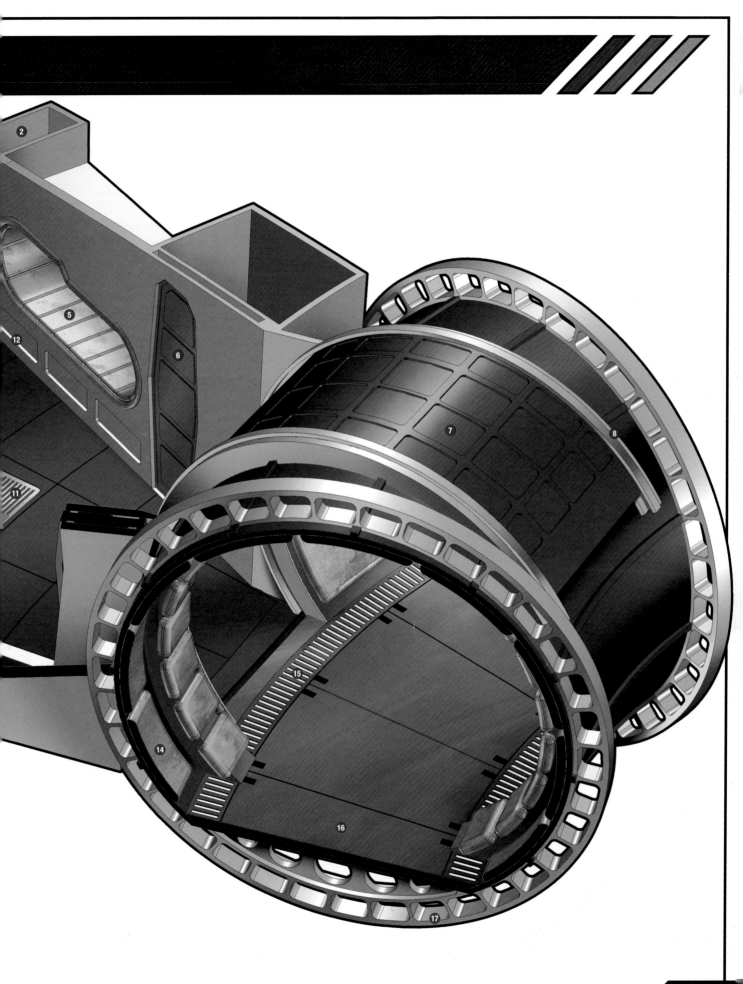

FIREFIGHTING APPARATUS

In addition to handheld fire extinguishers in the cockpit and near every hatch, the *Millennium Falcon* has an automated network of built-in firefighting apparatus. In the event of fire, the *Falcon*'s computer triggers pressurized canisters to spew anti-incendiary gas and high-expansion suppression foam (also known as firefoam) through a series of nozzles that are strategically positioned throughout the ship. Because of the *Falcon*'s age and temperamental computer systems, the automated firefighting outlets are sometimes unreliable and must be inspected frequently.

MEDPACS

Medpacs, also known as medi-packs, are emergency medical kits used to treat minor injuries and stabilize injured patients until they can be brought to advanced medical facilities. Stored in compartments throughout the *Millennium Falcon*, each medpac contains a variety of medicines and standard emergency-care tools, such as vibroscalpels and flexclamps, along with synthflesh and bacta patches.

The Chiewab GLiS (General Life-Sustaining) medpac holds supplies for treating contusions, broken bones, burns, and traumatic injuries. The GLiS also contains a diagnostic scanner to monitor a

patient's vital signs, a computer that stores treatment procedures, a bone stabilizer, and several spray splints that immobilize and protect broken bones. Standard medicines include coagulants to stop bleeding, healing salves and sterilizers to treat burns, and antiseptic irrigation bulbs to cleanse wounds and prevent infections.

The *Falcon* also has a supply of military-issue BioTech FastFlesh medpacs, which contain body chemistry boosters and advanced synthe-nutrient replicators that sustain patients with vital nutrients. The FastFlesh medpac also includes a sonic scalpel, a laser cauterizer, and nerve and tissue regenerators.

BREATH MASKS

The *Millennium Falcon* carries several sets of Gandorthral Atmospheric Roamer-6 breath masks, portable and inexpensive air purifiers that allow the users to breathe safely in a wide range of environments, from near vacuum to poisonous atmospheres. The mask fits over the user's nose and mouth, and is connected by a tube to a cylinder that houses a compressed air supply and purifier, a series of air scrubbers that filter out dangerous gases, dust particles, and other microscopic contaminants. The mask has an adjustable strap, and the small gas filter can fit in a pocket or be clipped to the user's belt. The mask also has a built-in comlink.

Although breath masks offer no protection from a total vacuum and do not shield users from corrosive atmospheres, they are effective in many emergency situations, as they prevent smoke inhalation and the spread of contagious airborne diseases. Because the Roamer-6 is cheap, versatile, and effective, it is standard issue on most starships and escape pods.

← The contents of a GLiS emergency medpac stabilize Luke Skywalker's wounds until he can be treated by a medical droid.

→ After traveling into a deep cavern on an asteroid, Chewbacca wears a Roamer-6 breath mask while inspecting the *Falcon*.

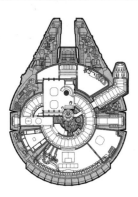

HOLOGAME TABLE

At Chewbacca's request, Han Solo installed a hologame table so that the Wookiee could play dejarik, a strategy game so old that its origins continue to generate debate among scholars and game aficionados. Manufactured by Lakan Industries, the late-model hologame table features a circular top with a radial-checkered surface, which rests upon a deck-mounted cylindrical column that houses a hologram generator. Control studs for power settings, data module insertion, and parameter settings are located on the table's outer rim.

In dejarik, two players control opposing teams of holographic creatures, also known as holomonsters, which are based on mythical and actual creatures from across the galaxy. A data module allows gameplay using either static or 'live action' pieces, and with different degrees of difficulty. In live-action mode, the holomonsters behave consistently with their inspirational

❶ **Game board**

❷ **Holo emitters**

❸ **Game state/
    scoring indicators**

❹ **Power settings**

❺ **Game mode select**

❻ **Support column**

❼ **Holo processor**

❽ **Table rotation control**

❾ **Control keys**

HOLOGRAPHIC CREATURES

❿ **Kintan strider**

⓫ **Ng'ok**

⓬ **Monnok**

⓭ **Molator**

⓮ **Mantellian Savrip**

⓯ **K'lor'slug**

⓰ **Ghhhk**

⓱ **Houjix**

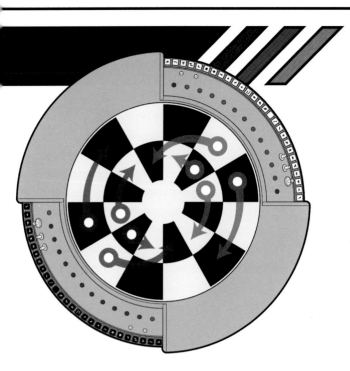

counterparts, and use their respective attributes—ranging from venomous stings and crude weapons to brute strength and supernatural powers—to wage war. As a holomonster moves across the table, it fights, maims, kills, and in some instances devours its opponents.

When not in use for gaming purposes, the durable hologame table also serves as an all-purpose table.

← ↑ In dejarik, two players each have four game pieces and attempt to eliminate all of their opponents in strategic attacks.

↓ ↘ Remotes can be configured to emit stun bolts, blasts of compressed air, non-lethal gases, beams of light, and even shrieking audio attacks.

COMBAT REMOTE

Han Solo keeps an Industrial Automaton Marksman-H combat remote for target practice aboard the *Millennium Falcon*. The remote has a small repulsorlift generator and eight maneuvering thrusters, allowing it to hover and move and turn swiftly through the air with instantaneous altitude adjustments. Like a droid, the remote possesses a degree of intelligence, but does not have any independent initiative, and acts on orders given by its owner. However, the remote's intelligence is relatively limited, drawing from a library of preprogrammed instructions and site-specific memories to complete basic tasks and functions. A handheld signaler controls the remote through high-pitch coded bursts.

Capable of firing two stun blasts per second, Solo's remote is programmed with numerous combat drills, each ending after a preset time or after a specific number of hits has been scored. After setting his blaster pistol to emit light only (not a destructive or stunning charge of energy), Solo fires at the remote, and its sensors automatically detect when a hit has been scored. The remote's stun blast intensity is variable, ranging from light discharges that merely tingle to full-intensity stun beams that can numb an organic target's limbs for several minutes. Although Solo is an expert shot, he finds the remote is excellent for practice at dodging attacks.

1 Fine maneuver thrusters	4 Programming transceiver
2 Target sensors	5 Repulsorlift drive
3 Repulsor vents	6 Emitter nozzle

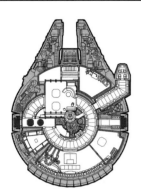

The *Millennium Falcon* has two docking rings, which are situated respectively on the port and starboard sides. Used to dock the YT-1300 to capital ships and space stations, the docking rings are sealed hatches with external magnetic couplings, and generally allow a smoother transfer of cargo than by way of the dorsal hatch. The docking rings can also be used to dock with transparisteel passenger gantries, which are generally found only at luxury spaceports.

Although both docking rings are the same size, the port-side ring has a much smaller airlock space because of the proximity of a second door. For this reason, the port ring sees less use. On one occasion, while Han Solo was transporting a motley group of passengers through hyperspace across the Corporate Sector, a passenger killed another in cold blood and then attempted to hide within the port docking ring's airlock. Because Han Solo's sympathies were very much with the killer's victim, and because the airlock's controls were within Solo's reach, the killer found himself removed from the *Falcon*.

⬇ Luke Skywalker and Lando Calrissian peer through the *Falcon*'s open dorsal hatch that is used to access the upper hull.

DORSAL HATCH

The *Falcon*'s port-side corridor also features an access port to the ship's dorsal hatch. A cylindrical tube pulls down from the ceiling while an elevating platform in the floor rises, carrying a single passenger through the upper layers of the hull; the cylindrical tube automatically locks to the elevated platform to create an airlock. The passenger rises out through an airlock hatch to arrive inside another ship's docking tube.

If the *Falcon* is surrounded by a pressurized atmosphere, one can also use this hatch to climb on to the ship's upper hull. Lando Calrissian used this dorsal hatch when he pulled Luke Skywalker into the *Falcon* when they fled Imperials on Cloud City.

UNIVERSAL DOCKING HATCH

The *Millennium Falcon*'s port-side corridor has a floor access to the ventral universal docking hatch. Although this hatch is indeed universal, in that it can lock on to most starship or starport docking rings and docking

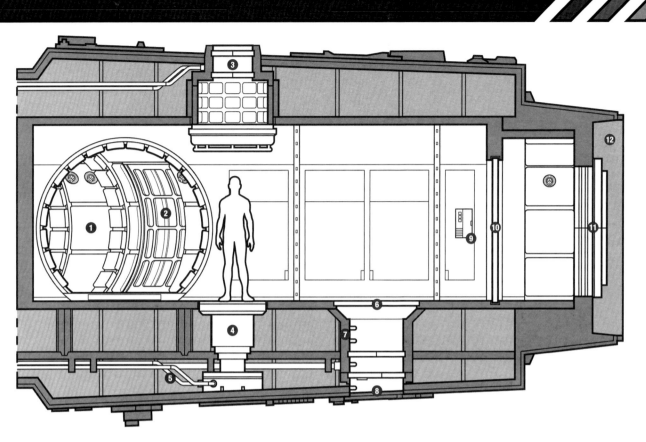

tubes, it was primarily intended for docking with small transports, specifically older vessels with cramped hatchways. Because Han Solo generally prefers to use the starboard docking ring for transferring cargo or boarding procedures, the ventral docking hatch is seldom used.

❶ Main corridor
❷ Hatch to crew quarters
❸ Dorsal hatch
❹ Elevating platform
❺ Hydraulic lines
❻ Floor access plate
❼ Ladder
❽ Universal docking hatch
❾ Airlock controls; lock release
❿ Inner airlock door
⓫ Outer door
⓬ Docking ring

← Descending through the lift tube located below the *Falcon*'s dorsal hatch, Lando Calrissian helps the injured Luke Skywalker into the ship.

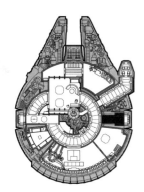

BOARDING RAMP

The original YT-1300f (freighter configuration) featured twin boarding ramps for the access of treaded cargo loaders and droids. These ramps extended beneath the port and starboard protrusions, in the same areas that the YT-1300p (passenger configuration) housed a pair of Class-6 escape pods.

The *Millennium Falcon* has a single hydraulically powered boarding ramp on the starboard side. This ramp angles upward toward the center of the ship when opened. When closed, it forms the floor of the passageway between the starboard docking ring and main corridor. A semicircular pressure hatch slides down from the ring corridor ceiling to seal the passageway and transform it into a large airlock. Shallow gear lockers set in the walls of the passageway contain a total of four folded environmental suits for excursions into dangerous atmospheres.

When Han Solo must meet with a client outside the *Falcon* during pickups and drop-offs, he and Chewbacca have their own signal system to communicate whether something is wrong. If Solo fails to give a subtle 'all's-well' signal as he and the client approach the boarding ramp, Chewbacca—seated in the cockpit—is prepared to fire the *Falcon*'s weapons at the client.

❶ **Locking studs**
❷ **Hydraulic actuators**
❸ **Exterior armor plate**
❹ **Foldout extension**
❺ **Manual controls**
❻ **Ramp**

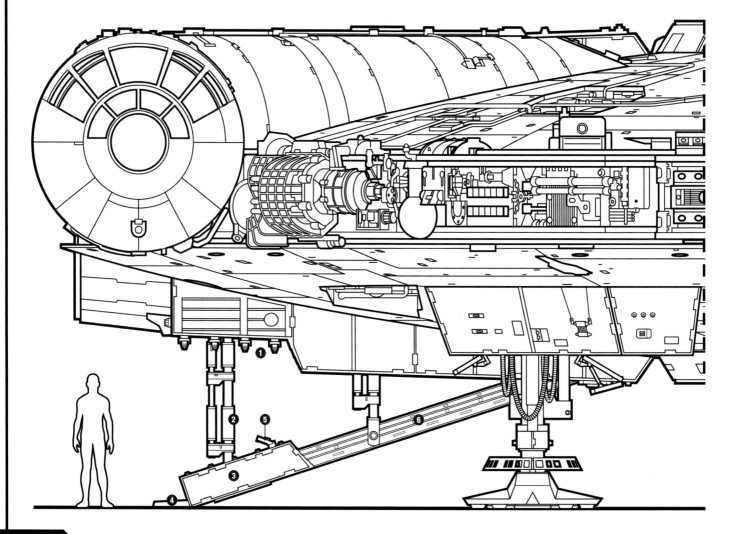

SECRET COMPARTMENT

The *Falcon*'s ring-shaped corridor is essentially a flat-bottomed circular tube, and is accessible to nearly every part of the ship's interior. Seven concealed, scanner-proof smuggling compartments, used for the safekeeping of valuable contraband, are built into the section of corridor that stretches between the boarding ramp passageway and the main hold. These compartments are covered by energy-absorbing plating and lined with exotic low-energy sensor jammers, which are capable of deceiving Imperial-issue full spectrum transceivers at far and close range; should passengers or crew hide within the compartments, Imperial scanners will not detect any life forms below the deck. The compartments lie close to the outer hull and can be vented into space in an emergency.

← A hatch in the *Falcon*'s tubular ring corridor leads to the boarding ramp. The corridor is lined with padding to minimize injury to passengers during turbulent flights.

← When the hatch is sealed, the boarding ramp chamber is transformed into an airlock.

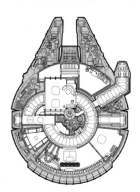

Escape pods are small space capsules capable of limited flight and maneuverability, and are typically located at key positions in a ship's hull to provide quick access in case of an emergency. After the escape pod is boarded, it is released via explosive separator charges and pneumatically or ballistically propelled from the ship. If the emergency occurs in deep space, the escape pod's crew must point the pod in the general direction of the nearest occupied planet or space lane, fire the rockets, and activate a distress beacon. Galactic law requires every ship—with the exception of small starfighters—to have enough pods to safely evacuate all crew and passengers.

➜ A rear view of an escape pod after explosive separator charges release the pod away from a larger ship and into space.

⬇ The escape pod's automated systems guide the pod to the nearest habitable world or space station.

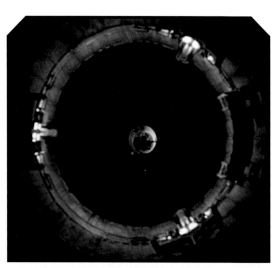

The YT-1300 was designed to carry a variety of Corellian Engineering Corporation-manufactured or CEC-compatible escape pods, ranging from single-passenger pods to multi-passenger lifeboats. When Han Solo acquired the *Millennium Falcon*, the ship carried five CEC Class-1 escape pods, each designed to carry a single passenger. The narrow confines of each Class-1 pod are padded to protect the occupant from injury. Although the flight control system in each pod is almost entirely automated, a compact built-in console has rudimentary controls that include a keypad, datascreen, and communications transceiver.

The datascreen displays sensor information for the nearest ships, planets, space stations, or space lanes, and the occupant can use the keypad to guide the pod toward a specific destination. The comm transceiver scans for activity on standard communication frequencies. If the passenger becomes unconscious, the pod's automated systems will activate a distress beacon and plot a course for a destination that has the most viable conditions for the passenger's survival. The pod also has an interior compartment for emergency supplies, including food rations and water, a survival shelter, medpac, breath mask, glow rods, and portable comm unit.

Han Solo and Chewbacca allow the possibility that the Class-1 pods might be useful for fellow travelers, but regard the pods as entirely impractical for themselves. They are too small for Chewbacca, and Solo cannot imagine abandoning either his co-pilot or the *Falcon*. Because the pods have only basic shield power and limited flight controls, Solo refers to them as 'space coffins'. Despite their disdain for the Class-1 pods, Solo and Chewbacca replaced a pod after an unwanted passenger, the skip-tracer Spray, launched one pod to the planet Ammuud.

Shortly after the destruction of the planet Alderaan, when the *Falcon* was snared by the Death Star's tractor beam, the Jedi Knight Ben Kenobi instructed Solo to dump some escape pods before the *Falcon* came into the Imperial battle station's close sensor range, while Luke Skywalker rigged the *Falcon*'s log so that it would deceive the Imperials into believing the crew had used the pods to abandon ship.

1. Atmospheric control vanes
2. Repulsor soft landing coils
3. Ingress/egress hatch
4. Emergency locator beacon
5. Sensor band
6. Hatch release
7. Emergency supplies storage
8. Attitude control thrusters
9. Retro-rocket nozzles (escape thrusters)

ESCAPE POD DRIVE SYSTEM

Like most escape pods, the CEC Class-1 pod has a simple drive system that holds just enough fuel to orient the pod toward the nearest habitable world and assist in emergency braking during landing. A simple repulsorlift drive unit is engineered to slow planetary descent and cushion landing, but if the repulsorlift fails the pod is also equipped with an emergency parachute and floatation devices.

SPECIFICATIONS

CRAFT:	CEC Class-1 escape pod
SHIELDING:	Equipped
ARMAMENT:	0
PASSENGERS:	1
CONSUMABLES:	5 days
COST:	5,000 (1,000 used)

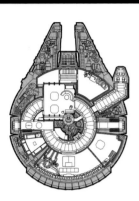

1. **Pressure helmet**
2. **Pull-down visor**
3. **Internal comlink**
4. **Helmet locking ring**
5. **Ship's registry patch**
6. **Chest pack straps**
7. **Pressure suit**
8. **Flak vest**
9. **Life support unit**
10. **Glove locking ring**
11. **Glove**
12. **Gear harness**
13. **Signal flares**
14. **Boots**

SPECIFICATIONS

NAME: **Immediac Model 10**
MANUFACTURER: **LifeLine Technologies**
FUNCTION: **Extravehicular activity**
OPERATING PRESSURE: **400hPa (5.8psi)**
LIFE SUPPORT: **8 hours, up to 4 days with larger tanks**

Spacesuits are sealed uniforms that possess an independent atmosphere supply, temperature regulators, and waste recyclers, which allow individuals to enter the vacuum of space for limited periods of time without harm. Spacesuits are available in nearly as many styles and sizes as there are space-faring species, but typically consist of a helmet affixed to a one-piece pressure garment, and allow survival for several standard days. Higher-priced spacesuits contain interior food supplies—usually dispensed through a tube in the helmet—that can further extend the survival period.

Because most spacesuits have heavy padding and insulation that can inhibit movement and dexterity, starfighter pilots generally prefer to wear lightweight vacuum suits, but spacesuits have the advantage of greater durability and longer-term atmosphere supplies.

For extravehicular repairs and emergencies, Han Solo wears a military surplus LifeLine Technologies Immediac Model 10 spacesuit. The suit's rear entry allows it to be easily donned in just under two standard minutes. The detachable helmet seals via a locking neck ring; it has a clear visor with an adjustable shade that reduces glare from reflected sunlight. A standard back-mounted canister provides life support for eight hours, but larger, interchangeable tanks can be added to extend the suit's duration up to four days.

Life-support controls can be adjusted on the box strapped across the spacesuit's chest. Gloves are secured by connecting lock rings on the wrists, which also allow the wrists to swivel. The palms of the gloves are textured to allow Solo to more easily grasp objects, turn knobs, and press switches and buttons. On the soles of the spacesuit's boots, electromagnetic grippers ensure a secure foothold against the ship's hull.

Han keeps his spacesuit stowed within a wall locker at the starboard airlock. Additional spacesuits and extravehicular equipment are also stored within the lockers of the port side airlock.

↑ Exterior repairs are always easier on solid ground. Work within hangar facilities whenever possible.

↓ Pressurized spacesuits aren't necessary when opening hatches in an upper atmosphere, but proper equipment and tether cables are recommended if a crew member goes out onto the hull.

SIZE COMPARISON CHART

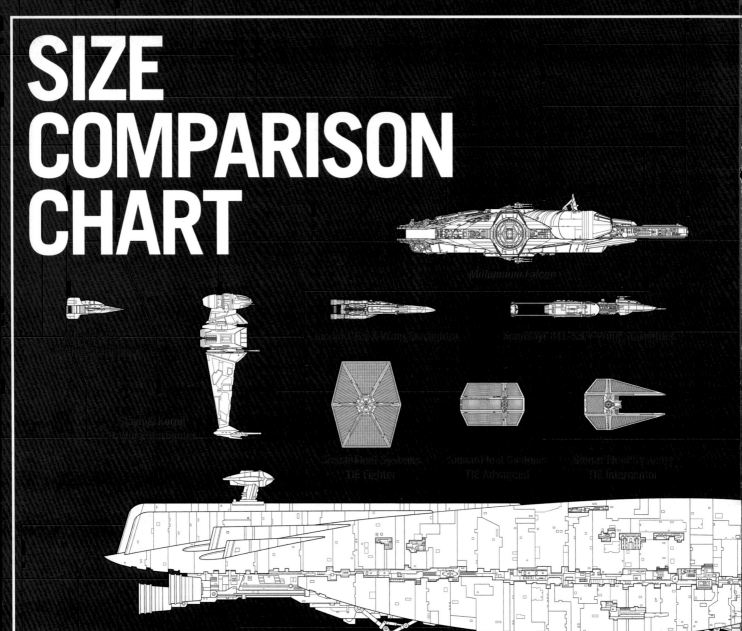

Millennium Falcon

Alliance 22
Y-Wing Starfighter

Slayne Korbit
B-Wing Starfighter

Incom T-65 X-Wing Starfighter

Koensayr BTL-S3 Y-Wing Starfighter

Sienar Fleet Systems
TIE Fighter

Sienar Fleet Systems
TIE Advanced

Sienar Fleet Systems
TIE Interceptor

Gallofree Yards Medium Transport

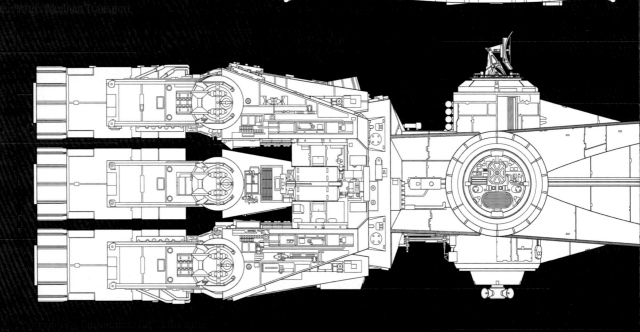

COMPARISON TO LARGER CAPITAL SHIPS

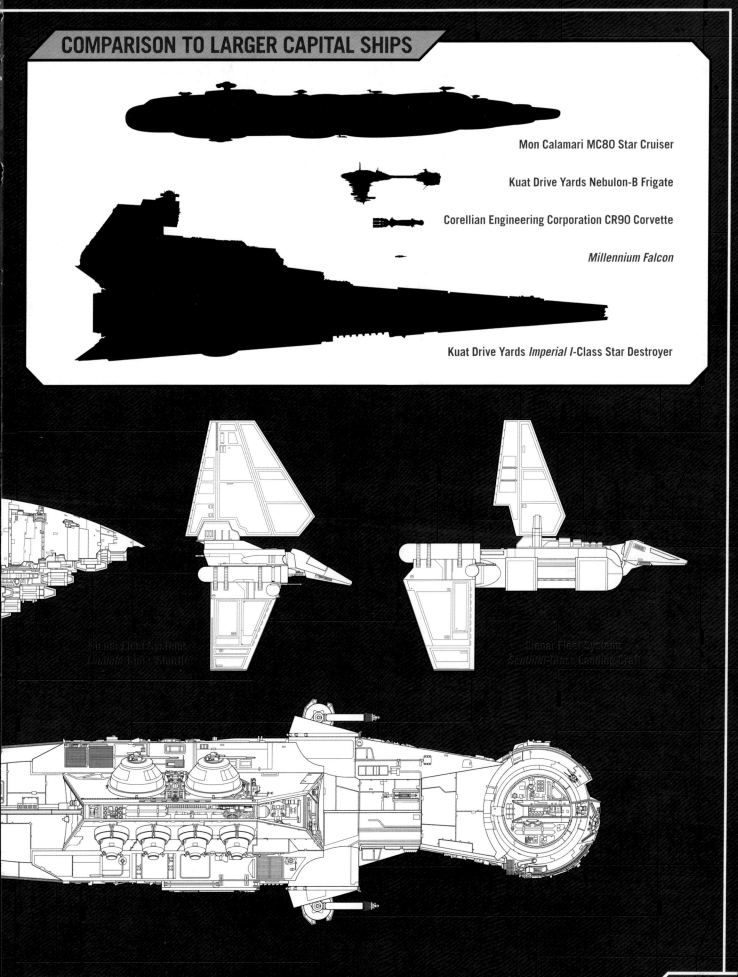

Mon Calamari MC80 Star Cruiser

Kuat Drive Yards Nebulon-B Frigate

Corellian Engineering Corporation CR90 Corvette

Millennium Falcon

Kuat Drive Yards *Imperial I*-Class Star Destroyer

Sienar Fleet Systems
Lambda-Class Shuttle

Sienar Fleet Systems
Sentinel-Class Landing Craft

ACKNOWLEDGMENTS

The author and artists of the *Millennium Falcon Owner's Workshop Manual* utilized information about the *Falcon* from many previously published *Star Wars* novels, technical manuals, and game books. Brian Daley's classic trilogy of Han Solo novels and James Luceno's novel *Millennium Falcon* were especially valuable. Attentive readers will note that many details from Luceno's novel are not mentioned in the *Owner's Workshop Manual*. This was not an oversight. The *Owner's Workshop Manual* covers the *Falcon*'s history up through *Return of the Jedi*, while the novel *Millennium Falcon* is set nearly four decades after *Jedi*, and begins with Han Solo still having much to learn about the *Falcon*'s history. If you have yet to enjoy the revelations in Luceno's excellent novel, you may do so without spoilers from us.

We are further indebted to the following writers and artists: Gary Astleford, W. Haden Blackman, Rob Caswell, Richard Chasemore, Greg Farshtey, Marc Gabbana, Jeff Grubb, Hans Jenssen, Shane Johnson, Paul Murphy, Thomas M. Reid, Mark Rein-Hagen, David West Reynolds, Brian Sauriol, Curtis Saxton, Peter Schweighofer, Bill Slavicsek, Bill Smith, Curtis Smith, Owen K. C. Stephens, George Strayton, Paul Sudlow, Rodney Thompson, Eric Trautmann, Raymond L. Velasco, Troy Vigil, Christopher West, Stewart Wieck, and Timothy Zahn.

We also gratefully acknowledge George Lucas, John Barry, Joe Johnston, Ralph McQuarrie, Lorne Peterson, Norman Reynolds, and their colleagues for their significant contributions to the *Falcon* in the *Star Wars* movies.

Special thanks to the following people for their help with reference for this project: Jeff Carlisle, Guy Cowen, Tim Effler, Shane Hartley, Barry Jones, Bryan Ono, Derek Smith and our friends at Lucasfilm including Leland Chee, Tina Mills, Brett Rector, and Jonathan Rinzler.